Venture

The Orla Series: Book 1

by

Darlene McCullough

Illustrated by Jenne Greaves

Edited by Jenne Greaves & Jennifer Steinhurt

D1522273

Published by Lulu.com

ISBN 978-0-557-17644-1

Acknowledgments:

Thank you to Kickstarter.com, all my "Kickers",
Johanna & Mike Kobran, Sharon & Jak Bestle,
David Marshall, Jenne Greaves, Jennifer Steinhurst,
Jiri Seger, John, and everyone who believed this was
a good idea.

For John: You make my
world magical every day

Contents

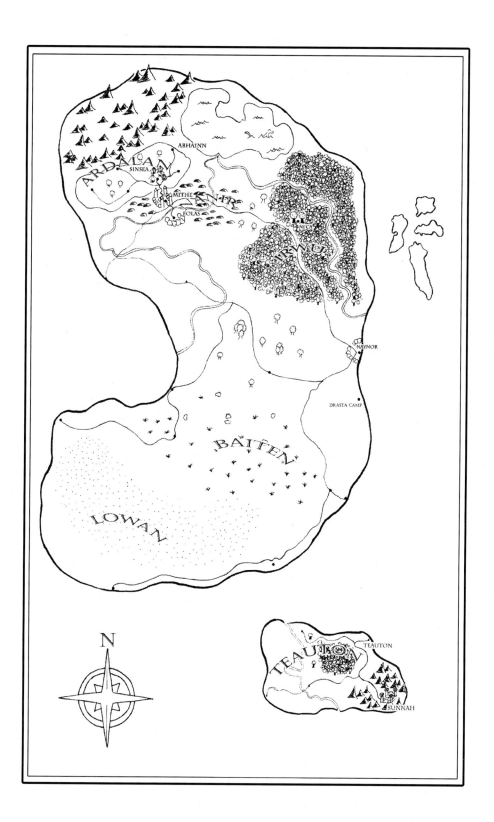

chapter One

It had been a long night staring at the eaves; listening to the sounds of the dark but not really hearing them. Some might say that she was lost in thought, though anyone who had spent a sleepless night in dread would know she had been thinking nothing at all. Her mind was blank with the emptiness of the task ahead of her; the loneliness that would soon consume her and a fear no amount of planning could shake. The effort required to keep her mind free had brought with it a dull headache that would follow her the rest of the day.

Just before dawn she rolled over and nuzzled her nose to the base of her husband's jaw, just below his beard. She took in a deep breath of his sweet, musky scent and kissed the nape of his neck. She drew in every sensation and tried to stretch the moments to bursting.

He stirred slightly and smiled in his sleep. He mumbled an

incoherent pledge to her and fell back to dreaming. She felt her lip quiver and her resolve falter. *I could stay here. He'd protect me.*

No! She silently demanded of herself. *Don't be a fool. You know better than that.*

She rose from their bed of straw and down and felt the coolness of the early morning creep up her nightdress and caress her knees. Gently as she could, she took her clothes to the next room, the only other room in their little cottage, and dressed.

She wrapped a few small items in cotton cloth and slipped them into her satchel. Securing her cloak quickly around her shoulders, she crept through the door and onto the path.

To an outsider it would seem that she was merely going to the market or making an early start on chores. They might not realize how early the hour was or notice the extra layer of clothes she'd put on.

Anyone from Sinsea that happened to see her would immediately recognize the change in routine, so she kept an ear alert for noises of anyone stirring. As far as she could tell she made it through the early morning silence unnoticed, and then beyond; through the fields and pastures. As the world got brighter she rounded the edge of next little village down the path and out into the woods.

She let the cottages fade into the distance behind her without a backward glance. Their occupants would soon stir and her husband would wake to find the other half of the bed empty. Orla wondered what would happen when he realized she was

2

gone. *Will be think a wild animal took me? That I got up in the night and got lost in the dark?*

She allowed herself to imagine the morning to come. Cian waking and calling her name; then getting up slowly, taking his time and thinking she was outside. Eventually, when she didn't return, he would start to look around and notice the things that were out of place. Finally, when he realized that coins were missing from the purse hanging by the door and their was food taken from the low cabinet, he would know. Orla didn't turn back because she was unsure she could keep going if she did.

The day began cold and crisp with the fresh air of spring; and though chill helped, Orla's headache persisted and she strained to focus and keep the necessary pace. She'd never been more than a few hours walk from her village and wanted to get beyond where anyone could recognize her as quickly as possible.

As the sun rose through the morning Orla untied the scarf from her head and let the long braid of her light brown hair fall down her back. Though she was pretty she had always thought of herself as plain and spent little time on her appearance.

It was too early in the year for merchants and travelers. Though she was on the main road Orla saw few people that morning and she was too anxious to slow down.

Early spring had brought with it steady rain for a few weeks which washed away the last of the snow and muddied the roads. Orla had begun to plan then, working out the details in her mind, and when the sun shone more over the last few days and the ground began to dry out she knew it was almost time to go. Yesterday was warm and sunny and she hoped today would be the same. Her window between the rainy season and the flood of merchants was short and it was time for her to go.

Orla tried to keep from reflecting on her past, but it was hard not to be sentimental. She was born and raised on the plateau and on her fifteenth birthday she was married to a weaver's son in Sinsea, the village next to hers. Her mother, father, and all her siblings had never been more than a few hours walk from their village. As far as she knew, the only person to ever wander was her grandfather.

Why would they ever want to leave? She wondered as she scanned the beauty of Ardlan, the plateau she'd always called home.

Fields stretched out to either side of the road and in a few weeks they would be full of wild flowers and farmers would be breaking up their tended plots. The harsh winds and heavy snows of winter had given way to a clear spring. Far in the distance the plateau dropped away to the hills of Nanir and mountains rose behind them.

Orla had not inherited her grandfather's desire to travel and explore. Ardlan was her home and now she was forced to leave it.

Having strayed so little in her life, Orla's plan didn't have many details. She knew from the merchants that visited during the summer that a sizable town bordered the plateau. From what they told her it was a heavy day's travel from her village and she needed to make it there tonight. While it was safe for a woman to walk the road in the day, she didn't want to risk sleeping outdoors.

Her plan was simple: she had to reach the town today. Then she could find a place to stay the night and work the rest out tomorrow.

Orla came to a crossroad and stopped. To the merchants the path cutting the road probably seemed like little more than an animal path, but Orla knew it led to a small village similar to hers. Orla's mother had brought her here just before she moved to Sinsea with Cain. They had come to visit her mother's sister and Orla spent the day playing with her cousins. They stayed so long that they spent the night and shared a mat with her mother. It was the only night she spent away from home until she she was married and this was the farthest she'd ever been from home.

She took a deep breath and continued, reminding herself that there wasn't time to waste on sentimental things.

In the early afternoon Orla broke for lunch. She was near to the edge of the plateau; below her the great rolling hills of Nanir fell away and she knew she was not far from her destination. The hills were blanketed with the light green grasses of spring and a few trees interrupted their gentle slope. She could see from the cliff's edge areas used for grazing and some patchwork of tended fields. She saw the road snake down the cliff side and off into a valley below.

Orla felt overwhelmed and diminished looking over such a wide, open sky. *How will I survive in this world I know so little about?* She'd been a simple weaver's wife; working beside him to make fabrics and baskets and knew nothing of exploring and travel.

Pushing her self-doubt aside, she stepped from the path to a more secluded grotto to give her mid-day thanks and knelt in a patch of grass.

As she knelt to give her praise to Danu for this day Orla was overcome. She finally had a moment's peace and it was too much for her. She lay down in the grass and the tears rolled from her eyes, so struck that she spoke aloud to herself. "I have nowhere to go". She knew no one in this great town.

She sobbed and heard no noise beyond her heavy breathing and sighs. She felt nothing beyond the heat in her face and pressure in her head. Behind the throbbing she wanted to reach out to Cian and be comforted, but he was not there. He never would be again. She was alone.

As the sobbing subsided, she tried to relax and regain her composure, but she could see it behind her eyes: the vision. The visions where the reason she fled; a demon's gift like nothing Orla had ever seen.

Orla had been as mischievous as any other child and as a

girl she occasionally snuck up to the huts of the wadima, medicine men who knew herbal remedies and advised the village on spiritual matters. Children rarely spoke or saw wadima unless they were ill; and were, therefore, fascinated with them.

Once, Orla pulled a loose seam aside on a cool summer night and watched the wadima brew an elaborate potion. It put him into a trance and he spoke with a council Orla could not see; he learned from the spirits how to cure an ailing child. That was the closest anyone in the villages ever came to visions. They were part of the rituals of the wadima and even for a medicine man a vision without the ritual was considered a bad omen.

Orla was no wadima and the new visions terrified her. She was afraid that something sinister grew within her; that the power she could feel channeling through her body was evil. She'd heard the stories from the old men who sat around drinking lager of villages who discovered one of their own had demon magic. The elders described how the possessed was beaten or stoned to protect the rest of the village from being infected with the demon.

This was why she fled. Orla left the village and would move where no one could recognize her. She would keep moving until she found a place large enough that she could go unnoticed and keep her secret. If no place like that existed she would find somewhere that she could be alone.

She couldn't even tell her husband, even the smallest child knew that her husband couldn't keep a secret.

The recollection of his strong body in their warm bed brought a fresh wave of grief over her. With her guard down the visions washed over her and began to pull her down. It was always there, and without concentration she couldn't keep it at bay.

What Orla saw through her mind terrified her. A great, powerful woman surrounded by inconceivable creatures that Orla could hardly bare to look at. They danced in fire and ice with the woman standing in the center, laughing. They called out in a language Orla didn't understand, beckoning to something or someone with their movements, throwing up their hands. Drums beat and music played from a band that Orla could not see and the dancers screamed their songs. She felt a dark energy coursing through the vision and the dancers, and it made her heavier. The rhythm pulled her down, down, into the darkness around them... then there was nothing.

chapter Two

Orla woke with a dry sensation in her mouth and was instantly afraid. *Where am I?* She lifted her head from her arms, feeling the pull of a muscle in her neck. Her whole body clenched with ache. Her hip hurt from digging into a rock.

She then recalled the flight from her home. After the poor night's sleep the previous evening she'd been pulled asleep with the weight of the vision. They always left her tired, but the fear accompanying this one made it especially exhausting. She looked up to see the sun was nearly across the hills. She'd heard the descent from the plateau was not easy or fast. She'd need to hurry if she was to have a safe place to sleep tonight.

The road here dropped quickly and switched back on itself. This winter had been wet and icy, and in places the way had crumbled to little more than a path. The larger merchants traveled with their own crews and would repair the roads, though they weren't expected for a few weeks.

Orla's clothes were well made but simple and her shoes were little more than leather slippers. A life spent sitting at a loom had kept her pleasantly plump and she had few calluses. She was not fit to be scrambling over rocks. Tripping and falling, skinning her knees and cutting her hands, Orla reached the bottom of the path.

Not far from the base of the hill many paths intersected in what soon became a wide road and houses began to cluster on either side. Other travelers cluttered the road, some with small carts and a few with horses.

The houses were different from the homes in her village, larger and more skillfully built. Many were raised from the ground on foundations of mortar and stone; some with porches and woodwork. Dusk was easing in. Orla turned a corner to discover a narrow valley below her and Mithe glimmering a short distance off.

Torches had been lit at the gate and her eyes widened to the sight. Mithe. It was as if every village she'd ever seen and every person she'd ever known had been gathered in one place. *How could a village get so large?* Orla continued to move down toward the gates as if in a trance, despite the self-doubt growing inside her.

What if this is a mistake? I'm no traveler. I should have trusted the elders of our village to do what is right. She tried to shut out her inner voice. There was no going back now, even if this had been a mistake. How could she explain her absence and what would she do when they found out her secret? *Just keep walking. I'll worry tomorrow.*

Until now Mithe was merely a legend to Orla, a collection of stories shared by the merchants who visited the village. These worldly, well-dressed men and their exotic wives had seen more exciting, wonderful things in a year than Orla could have hoped to experience in a lifetime. Their tales of massive cities, other species, strange foods, and even rumors of magic would terrify and excite her. Most of the villagers believed it to be exaggeration at best, but a part of Orla always thought it was true, even if she never admitted it.

Here she was, before the gates of the great town. Try as she might she couldn't rationalize away her fears; this place was so big and she was so simple. She had no plan and no idea where to go. Falling in with others coming into the town the guards paid no notice to her; she was nearly invisible in the crowd.

Beyond gates taller than the largest watch towers she'd seen at home, cobbled streets were flanked by stone houses. She marveled at the construction of solid stone buildings with second floors. Shops of all kinds were closing up for the night and she saw signs depicting everything from armor and fabric to fresh fish and fruit, and some she didn't recognize.

She followed the flow of the other travelers to a great square lit with torches on high poles. A young man was walking the streets and lighting them one by one with a flick of his hand. Orla gasped with shock. *Magic! It's true!* Here before her was proof that the merchants did not lie.

She'd seen the wadima make simple potions or mutter enchantments over the sick and injured. These spells and the knowledge of plants was passed from one wadima to the next as a smithy from father to son or a loom from mother to daughter. There were rumors of greater magic; though most in her village believed it could only be harnessed by sprites and demons.

Here, though, was someone who harnessed the elements: controlling fire with the ease of raising a glass.

After a few moments she came back to herself, realizing that no one else was watching this young man and she felt her face burn. She alone had stood there in astonishment as he gestured at a lamp and moved on to gesture at the next as easily as if he were sweeping the floor. Orla told herself that she would keep such blatant reactions of wonder under control; though she fully expected something else to grab her attention before long.

The square had emptied while she was watching the lamp lighter; she had been following the other travelers and didn't know what to do next. Her heart began to flutter in her chest and her mouth started to dry. Up until now all she'd had to do was walk; but standing in the square, with nowhere to go and wanting desperately not to stick out, she struggled to keep her mild panic at bay.

On the far end of the square she heard the loud noise and cheers of people gathering. She'd been to larger villages, like Abhainn, and eaten in the open air stalls of the fishermen. This seemed like a similar place to gather and eat, so she followed the sound to the windows. Inside some of the other travelers she had entered Mithe with sat and drank.

The inn was rowdy and full, and despite her reservations Orla had little choice. She went in and stood beside the door, watching.

Large men drank and sang in the main room. A few large round tables at the center were flanked by shorter square tables with rough cut benches whose tops had been worn smooth by years of use. The short bar held only three stools and a handful of servants bustled back and forth between the bar, kitchen, and tables. There was plenty of open space; only a few men were in the tavern, though they made enough noise for dozens.

"Hallo. You need somethan?" A short, round woman with a few empty glasses in front of her called from behind the bar. Orla stood dumbly near the door, too tired to reason and trying to take the woman in. She was only a few years older than Orla and had long, dark hair that fell across her shoulders in lose, ragged curls. More of her skin was exposed than Orla had ever seen of a woman in public. She spoke again, loudly.

"Can ya hear me? Do ya speak? I said 'do ya need anythin'?'" Orla was snapped from her fog and made her way to the bar.

"Yes. Do you have rooms?"

"Well, it's an inn i'd't it? Ya wantin' a place ta' stay?"

"Yes."

"Come on through that door. We'll get'cha set up." The dark haired woman motioned to another door on the far end of the bar.

Orla entered a darker room with a counter and waited. The walls were well cut stone, the same dull gray as the cliffs near by, and the floors rough wood. In front of the counter the floor was worn smooth like the benches in the tavern. After a few moments the door behind the counter opened and Orla could see what looked like a kitchen beyond. The dark haired woman entered.

"Surry fur the wait. Ma normal help's tak'n the night off 'n didn't ask fur it. Do ya know how long y'll be here?"

"I'm not sure."

"S'all right. Anyone else be sharing wi'ch ya?"

"No. A room by myself, please."

"A room wit'a lock fur ya then. Should'I send someone up with ya supper?" Orla hesitated. She was very tired and was having trouble keeping up.

"I'll take it with me."

"Alright. I'll get it and show ya up."

"Umm..." Orla hesitated and the woman turned back.

"Ya?"

"I. Aah. Is this your place?"

"Ah! How rude'a me. I'm Mirna and this is ma place," The woman stuck her hand out to greet Orla and she took it awkwardly. "And you are?"

"Orla." Mirna paused a moment waiting for Olra to say more, and when she didn't Mirna nodded slightly.

"Well then, I'll show ya to yur room."

The woman left through the door to the kitchen and came back with a bowl of soup and crusty bread. Smelling the soup, Olra realized she wasn't just exhausted, but also starving. Orla followed the woman to the main room and hesitated when she cut through the noisy crowd. Orla was too tired to be brave and had never been surrounded by a group of strangers; she avoided the revelers and mounted the stairs quickly. Mirna showed her a small room just past the top of the stairs. Orla thanked her, took the soup, and locked the door the moment the woman left.

The room was the same rough stone and wood as the office and tavern. On the outside wall was a small bed for one and next to the door was a larger table with a basin of water. Besides the quilt and pillow on the bed the room was empty.

Orla sat on the edge of the bed and stared down at her soup. She was numb from the day and the sensation of the warm bowl in her hands felt wonderful. She sipped the soup slowly and as it rolled down her throat the warmth penetrated the fog inside her. As the ate, Orla started to worry.

She worried about her gold running out and becoming a beggar. She worried she'd never see Cian again. She worried about safety of this place. She started to worry that she wouldn't be able to sleep with all her worrying.

The soup gone and, setting the bowl aside, she went to the basin to washed the dust from her face and hands. With this

15

small normal action she felt the weight of the day. Orla lapsed into a fitful sleep as soon as she lay down despite the laughter below in the tavern.

Chapter Three

Light filtered through brown stained window next to the bed and Orla woke from a thick sleep. She'd been so tired she slept in all her clothes and her jaw was tight from clenching it in her sleep. She lay in the straw bed and stared at the rough-hewn ceiling. Uneven straw stuck in her side through the fabric cover of the mattress but she did not move.

What now?

Orla's entire life until yesterday had been encompassed in a few small villages. She was born and raised in a small village too small for a name. Her parents were kind and she played and worked with her many siblings and the other children of her village. Though she knew little of her father's business she'd seen him help local smiths and farmers making deals with merchants and resolve disputes when they arose.

She passed from her family's care to a good match with her husband, Cian. He was gentle, kind, and saw them as equals. She moved to be with him in the village of Sinsea, named in the local dialect for the sweet ginger-grass that grew near by. He taught her his weaving trade and they flourished. She had a natural hand for finer fabrics and he produced the stronger, rougher canvas they could sell in bulk to passing merchants. They were happy and she was fortunate to have a husband, a home, and a few rare luxuries. During the day they were great friends and business partners, and at night they would lie together as lovers.

Danu damn you! None of that matters now. Get up or you'll end up in the gutter after they kick you out.

Orla forced herself from bed, stripped naked, and cleaned herself in the cold water from the basin. Her journey had been long and dirty.

She hadn't brought much and laid what she had on the bed: two shirts, two long skirts, an extra pair of undergarments, and one pair of plain leather shoes. She had a light overcoat and a scarf for her hair. The fruit and crackers hadn't lasted long on the road so she would need to buy food. She dressed in the more durable of her outfits, folded the other clothes, and hid them beneath her pillow.

If she didn't find work today or tomorrow she wouldn't be able to afford another night at the inn. She tried to make a plan but none of her ideas seemed reasonable; without money to buy a loom and thread she couldn't weave. Even if she could, Cian was bound to hear from merchants about the woman making fine fabrics nearby.

No, she needed a way to make more gold and then she would move on.

After dressing she headed down to the tavern for the morning meal. The dark haired woman, dressed more modestly with her hair tied back, was serving a plain porridge. The tavern was nearly empty and Orla sat at one of the circular tables near the bar. At the table by the window the only other patrons, two men, were talking. They made no effort to keep the conversation to themselves.

Orla tried to keep her eyes on her bowl, but from the corner of her eye she watched the one facing into the room. He had a roughly shaven beard and a scar on his left cheek. The other had his back to her and seemed too short to be human. The taller one was speaking:

"Marin asked me to get a few together...apparently there's an infestation. I would have liked to know an hour ago, now everyone has left for the day."

He glanced up and saw her listening. Orla froze, afraid what he would say when he realized she'd been eavesdropping. She wasn't trying to be rude but they were the only ones there.

"You there. Know how to hold a sword?"

Orla choked on her porridge and tried not to spit it back onto the table; she took a moment to swallow and then found her voice. "No. I'm better with a dagger...or a bow for hunting."

"You can hunt?"

"I have before, yes." The shorter man turned to see her and Orla tried no to stare again when she realized he was definitely not human. He was shorter and wider than any man she'd seen. His brow was thicker and longer and every bit of him above the collar, other than his face, was covered in rough, dark auburn hair. The top was kept short and a beard was tucked into a band that ran diagonally across his chest. Orla tried to focus on what the taller man was saying, but missed it entirely. "I'm sorry. What?"

"You need work? You for hire?"

"Yes!" Orla tried to be calm, but she was excited by her good fortune. She straightened and tried to look tough and knowledgeable. "I'll be here for a while. What kind of work do you have in mind?"

The short, hairy one glanced at his companion before answering and Orla thought he was smiling beneath his beard.

"Extermination." From the shorter one, his voice deep and gruff.

"Of what?"

"Well, we'd start you on something easy and move you up if you don't die."

Orla's eyes got big and he let out a rough and hearty laugh that seemed to make the board in the floor bounce a little.

"Lighten up!" The larger one said as he stood and walked to her table. He slapped her shoulder in what was intended as a reassuring gesture. "No one's died yet. I'm Darragh and this is

20

Ternell. We'll be working with you. Don't worry, lass, we wont let anythin' happen to ya."

She reached forward to take Darragh's hand, trying to keep her own from trembling. "Orla. Yes, I'll take the work."

"Excellent!" He took her hand and gave it a shake and if it quivered, he didn't notice. "We just need one more and we'll be on our way. Mirna!" He called into the back, behind the counter, "Is your nephew about today? We could use him."

"He should be out back." Came the voice of the dark haired woman floating from the kitchen.

"I'll just be a moment." Darragh strode from the room through a back door. He returned with a boy of less than eighteen in his wake, walking quickly to keep up.

"This is Lorcian." The boy nodded to Orla with a smirk. "Right then, let's get to work."

Darragh and Ternell lead them through the city, which was now bustling with a day already begun. Try as she might, Orla couldn't contain the urge to glance and stare at everything. It seemed even the cobblestones at her feet were buzzing with the energy of the plaza.

In the early morning hours carts had rolled in and stalls opened. Gems and coins were being traded for goods of all sorts and the warm smells of incense and cooked meats rolled out of side streets and stores like a delicious fog. Men and women in armor and robes bickered over the prices of things Orla had never heard of. There were even a few races here that she had never seen.

A large creature covered in scales and armor argued loudly with a small, slight female that her prices were robbery. Despite herself, Orla stopped and gaped at the scene. *How is she not afraid?* She leaned around to look at them both.

"Never seen a drastra before?" Orla startled. Darragh had crept behind her, unnoticed, and spoke in her ear.

"No," she uttered, and he looked her square in the face.

"Have you been to Mithe before?"

Orla looked to her feet on the cobbles and blushed full in the face. *Am I so obvious?* "No," she mumbled.

Darragh stepped back now and looked her up and down. Orla looked up at him, unsure what he could possibly be looking for. He leaned in again.

"You have very pretty eyes. I didn't notice in the dark." Her face burned crimson and she felt it reach the top arch of her ears. Many people told her that her eyes were an unusual blue. They were deep with lighter flecks throughout and special for someone born so far north. It felt too intense from this man in this place, out in the open-air market where anyone could hear.

"Well then." Darragh broke the moment and raised his voice. To Orla's surprise he strode toward the stall with the drastra! "Chusa!" he called across the courtyard. "How fares this day?"

The scaly behemoth turned and Orla could see him clearly now. He towered over Darragh by more than a head and was even broader than Ternell. In place of hair he had a ridge that started between his eyes and was centered over the top of his head.

His eyes were narrowed at either end and the irises were a muddy orange. The lower half of his face was a short snout with slits at the end for nostrils. When he saw Darragh his lips parted, in what Orla assumed was intended as a smile, and revealed yellowed teeth. Some were broken, though most were sharp.

"Darragh!" His loud voice was accompanied by a rumbling in his chest that startled Orla. "I'm well, my friend." He reached forward and slapped Darragh on the shoulder. "Looking for some supplies, if I could find an honest price." The drasta turned toward the merchant and Orla caught the flick of a thin tail she hadn't noticed before. The ridge on his head ran into the top of his armor and out to the tip of the tail.

"Good day Darragh." The merchant's voice was like icicles playing against one another and Orla turned her attention from Chusa at the gently pleasing sound, wanting to hear more. If Chusa was the largest creature Orla had ever seen, this merchant was the opposite.

She was slight and her neck and arms were elegantly long and thin and seemed out of proportion in length. Her skin was slightly blue, like lips on someone who was in the cold to long, and had a waxy luster. Her hair was pale, almost white, and shined in the sun. Below thick lashes, round eyes that were larger than a humans stared out; they were a dark navy, almost purple, with light blue flecks that reflected the light and made her huge eyes shine.

Orla unconsciously leaned in, hoping to hear the musical

23

voice again.

"Good day, Faye." Darragh dipped his head to the merchant. "I hope you're not being too much of a cheat." Darragh turned and motioned to Orla with a crooked smile. "I'd like you to meet a new friend of mine."

Orla was rooted to the ground for a few beats of her heart and then caught her toe as she stepped forward. As she righted herself Darragh leaned in to Chusa and whispered loudly "Be nice. She's not met one of your kind before."

"Then why should I lie to her like that?"

"Orla, meet Chusa of the Drastra and the Nixie Faye."

Orla greeted them each in turn but said little else. She tried to be subtle while she studied these creatures that stood like humans but seemed so little like them. Darragh spoke with briefly, though Orla wasn't able to keep her attention to the conversation.

"We should be off. There's work to do." Darragh said, breaking through Orla's awe. "Come on, Orla."

Orla nodded to each of her new acquaintances and followed Darragh. Her mind skipped around, trying to keep up with this new information.

"I thought they behaved well," Darragh said, smiling down at her.

Orla was unsure if this was a joke or not. She smiled weakly, not wanting them to think she had no humor, and hurried behind the others.

They turned off the main avenue and through neighborhoods she hadn't seen the night before. Through a residential district where small children were playing, the occasional baby could be heard. Orla did her best to push the sound from her mind.

The cramped houses gave way to businesses and, as they got closer to the river, to warehouses. Darragh relaxed his pace to bring them all up to speed.

"The town's larderer has asked for our help. The warehouse holding the dry good for the militia has been infested and if it isn't resolved soon they won't be able to feed their men." He stopped in front of a large door and turned. "That's why we're here."

Orla meekly asked, "What's the infestation of? Rats?"

"Worse. Imps." Darragh turned around and grabbed the handle of the doors. "They're easy enough to deal with. Just root them out from behind things and stab them." He hesitated, and turned from the doors to Orla. "You do have a weapon?"

"Umm...no. Sorry."

Lorcian, the inn-keepers nephew, gave an involuntary snort and Darragh shot him a look that said 'Be quiet' and stepped toward Orla. He reached down to his boot, never removing his eyes from her face, and handed her a wooden handled dagger.

"Thank you."

Darragh made a sound and face that could have been a laugh or an annoyed release of air. He turned back to the doors and peeked over each shoulder.

"Ready?"

When no one said otherwise, Darragh flung the doors open and stepped in. Ternell and Lorcian followed while Orla hesitated at the door. At first everything was quiet. They moved among the crates and waited, but nothing happened. Orla felt safety in silence and stepped into the cool dark of the warehouse.

An explosion of noise and action began. The double doors behind them slammed shut and a pile of wheat sacks was pushed over, the top bag ripping and scattering grain across the packed earthen floor.

Orla stood stone still as clatter filled the room around her. Dozens of creatures, knee high and all different colors, seemed to come from within the walls. They had long arms, much longer than their legs, with a thick bicep but thin forearm. They seemed to pop from place to place, appearing out of nowhere.

Darragh was skewering as many as he could with his sword and not bothering with the effort of picking them off, as Ternell tried to knock them out with his hammer, and Lorcian sprung down an isle between shelves with a short sword drawn.

After a stunned moment Orla swiped her dagger at the nearest one and missed. It giggled and leapt in the air, making faces as it hovered before her. In her distraction Orla didn't notice the other imps sneaking up around her. When she realized they were tugging her clothing it was too late. Orla took a few clumsy swipes with the dagger, but lost her balance as the imps teamed up and lifted her from her feet.

Higher and higher toward the ceiling they lifted her, as

others imps came to help. Some pinched her face, neck, and legs and they all giggled and taunted her. Darragh, Ternell, and Lorcian stood below her, unable to help beyond the reach of their swords. Orla began to scream and shake, begging for help. The imps began to toss and drop her, twisting her limbs and biting her.

In a flash of light, with a great scream of desperation, Orla felt an explosion of energy around her. She felt herself expand and didn't know what was happening. Time slowed for her and she was bathed in an orange glow and the biting and pinching suddenly stopped. She was confused, but thankful for whatever had stopped the imps.

To the men on the ground it looked as if Orla burst into flames. They all froze, and an instant later the roasted bodies of imps began falling around them. One fell on the face of the stunned Darragh, bringing him back to sense. Ternell was perfectly placed to break Orla's fall as she came crashing to the ground; unsinged though covered in imp-bite welts.

After climbing off of Ternell, Orla stood and stared at the three men, hoping one of them could explain what just happened. They stared back. Her eyes were wide and her hair standing up. They gaped with open mouths at one another in silence, everyone waiting for something. As it began to dawn on Orla that none of her three companions caused the explosion, and what that meant, she felt the familiar blush reach her face and looked down to the floor.

"Good job, new girl!" Lorcian slapped her on the back.

Ternell stepped up to her as well.

"Why didn't you tell us you were a wizard? We could use that kind of help."

"Wizard?" Orla was stunned; *Is that what they think just happened!?* "I'm no wizard." Orla looked at each of them, completely dumbstruck. "I don't think I could do that again if I tried."

"That's never happened before?" Darragh looked into her face as if watching for a lie.

"No. Never." Orla was convinced that they were mistaken and did her best to convince herself of it as well. She had enough problems between visions and running away, she wasn't prepared to add bursting into flames to that list.

Darragh replied with a grunt and looked around the warehouse. The tops of some of the stacks were smoldering, but nothing seemed seriously damaged. He began to search the stacks, looking for any remaining imps. It seemed that most of them had come to join the fun of harassing Orla though one or two were found untying grain bags or digging holes near the foundation. Darragh quickly disposed of the remaining imps and instructed his team to wait for him at the inn.

Orla followed Ternell back and Lorcian said he'd meet them later.

Orla didn't want to talk much on the walk to the inn; though she didn't want to be left with her own thoughts either. Ternell was friendly, and though Orla dodged his questions about her own life he was willing to share his own stories.

He was from a region far to the south near the bottom of the world called Teauton; born and raised in a capital of the same name. He described to her the great mountains of the far south and the temples to Sunnah his people had built at the highest peaks. He continued with fine detail about the cities carved into the mountains themselves.

Orla felt more comfortable with the strong, little man the more he talked, and as they reached the inn she dared to ask her first question of the walk.

"Isn't it horribly cold there?"

Ternell gave a hearty laugh, as Orla was learning he was likely to do.

"I'm a dwarf! We are built not to mind the cold!"

A dwarf! Another creature? How is it we were only on the far side of the plateau and never heard of them?

As if reading her mind, Ternell spoke up.

"There aren't many of us that live so far north. We like to trade, but we like being with our own kind too."

"How did you get here then?"

"Well, it's normal for my people to have many children, each in the birth order has a place in their family and their clan. The first is expected to learn the family trade, inherit the family home, and care for the elders as they age. The second is often married to the first of another family to strengthen ties. The third is expected to learn a new trade that is not currently represented in the clan and family, and the fourth to apprentice with someone who did not have children or their children died. This way all the roles are filled and the clan flourishes, bringing merit to each family. Each successive child filling a less-needed role.

"Most families stop at four, making a fifth child rare and special. The fifth child is to go out into the world and learn all that they can: making new connections and trade routes, learning new crafts and skills. There were only two fifth children in my generation." Ternell paused a moment and his tone changed from one of description to one of reverence, "One fell into a ravine just as she reached her maturity." He reached up and stoked his beard, then looked to Orla and continued.

"I am the other. That's why I am here. When I return home it will be with fresh knowledge and for the betterment of my clan. My entire generation is reliant on my success, and when I return it will be to marry a widow and raise a family of my own."

A silence fell between them for a few moments and Orla heard the mid-day bell toll.

"Oh." Orla started, and inquired where she might find a temple to Danu or a park.

"Mirna keeps a shrine to Danu in the courtyard at the back. I'll be taking my prayers in my room. Be back here when you're done, Darragh is expecting us." With that Ternell gestured to a door and turned toward the stairs.

Orla let herself through to the courtyard and joined Mirna before the shrine, but had little mind for prayers with the events of the day. Curious that a dwarven warrior keeps noon prayer. *I wonder who he'd pray to with an ax like that...* Her mind drifted from one thought to the next, only going through the physical motions of worship as she did in her childhood. *I wonder if Cian is looking for me.* She blinked away a rogue tear. *What's happening to me? What was that fire? Am I in danger if any of them tell?* Mirna didn't seem to notice her distraction; perhaps it was the foreignness of praying with someone new.

After a final swoop of her arms and a low prostration Orla returned to the tavern to wait for Darragh.

Orla and Ternell didn't wait long. Lorcian joined them and soon after Darragh returned and paid them each a days wage of three gold coins. Orla beamed. She'd never made this much in one day of weaving and it meant she would be fed and sheltered for at least a week.

They spent the rest of the afternoon and evening in the tavern, telling stories and drinking ale. Orla didn't speak much, preoccupied with thoughts of home and not wanting to give too much of herself away to men she barely knew.

Darragh wasn't speaking much either. He laughed occasionally and followed the conversation, but seemed distracted.

After everyone had supped and the thought of bed was creeping in, he left with few words.

That night Orla lay awake, her body exhausted from the unexplained inferno and her mind overwhelmed with new information. In the silence of the late night her ears buzzed.

I can't believe I've gotten this far, and I'm safe now; but what did I get myself into?

She closed her eyes and saw Cian as if he were far in the distance. A tear welled up and she tried to bring his face into focus. She was running - running along the plateau and trying to reach him. He was raising his arms up to greet her. She relaxed into his arms and felt the safe warmth of home. They were about to kiss, when suddenly their cottage burst into flames. Cian was too close and his back was burnt. He cried out in pain.

Orla gasped herself awake, covered in sweat. Her hands felt hot and she leapt from the bed. She was across the room in two strides and when she plunged her throbbing hands into the basin a light steam rose. She looked at the straw bed and thanked Danu that it hadn't burst into flames in her sleep.

Orla grabbed the down pillow and blankets and settled into the floor, determined not to burn the inn down on her second night.

Chapter Four

For a few days Orla fell into a routine. She woke in the morning when the sun reached her eyes, joined Mirna for breakfast, explored a part of the city she had not yet visited, and sought out Darragh to see if there was any work.

Darragh and his group provided many services for a variety of people in Mithe: guarding special packages, killing rats that invaded warehouses, and exterminating small magical creatures that threatened near-by farms. Orla was beginning to use her dagger with more confidence and Lorcian was giving her lessons in the afternoons when they weren't working.

When Orla forgot to worry enjoyed the routine, though at night she was reminded in her dreams that she couldn't stay long. She saw Cian and different things she loved burning. She'd wake from the nightmares and reach to him for comfort, finding nothing.

Terrified of bursting into flames as she slept, Orla had taken to smearing mud on her hands and wrapping them in wet cloths before going to sleep; a practice that the women cleaning her room surely loathed. Orla felt guilty about the inconvenience, but decided that burning the inn to the ground would be much worse. So far she liked the bustling town and didn't want to leave; so she let the lack of a next step convince her to stay.

Ten days after her arrival, Orla woke up earlier than she'd expected. This particular morning the visions were especially hard to fight and she wasn't able to sleep. The night before she'd dreamed more about earth than fire, and attributed this to her mud-wrapped hands.

Orla washed and dressed and went down to meet Mirna; she had gotten into the habit of helping with the dishes and other simple chores, missing the duties of her own home. In return, Mirna occasionally had an egg or some local fruit waiting for her at breakfast. This morning it was a spiky, hard skinned fruit with an orange pulpy center from the south. Mirna called it a nanga and Orla ate it gladly.

With the warm weather merchants had begun to stream in and out of Mithe. They came into town dirty and tired from the road and spent the fresh gold from their trades in Mirna's tavern. Orla sat to one side, enjoying the nanga and watching for Darragh or Ternell to arrive with work.

When neither arrived, Orla set out for a walk. They hadn't been around in two days, though with enough gold to keep her for four more days she's wasn't worried. With little else to do, she wanted to explore.

At the armory she saw Chusa, the drasta she'd met her first day. His leathery-green skin no longer startled her, though his teeth were just as sharp as that first day. He'd never given her a reason to be wary, but Orla gave him a wide birth after a general greeting.

She moved on, past the weapons shop where she'd purchased her own dagger so she could return Darragh's, the clothing shop where she'd replaced her simple village garments for clothes that were better suited to move and fight with, and a cafe where she tasted a warm, sweet, syrupy beverage from the far east for the first time. Orla was getting used to the city life quickly, finding that it suited her better than she'd thought it could.

Orla came around the corner to the city square and to the stall of Faye, the Nixie she'd met her first day in Mithe. Being less threatening than the drasta, Orla greeted her warmly.

Faye's stall was filled with all types of items Orla recognized the pieces of, but didn't understand why they were so expensive. Bits of polished wood with precious metals and stones fastened to them, some clothes and fine jewelry, there was even some armor and weapons set to the back of the stall.

"They're enchanted," Faye said in her quiet, clear, musical voice. Her words seemed to float to Orla's ears. "You're Darragh's new companion, is that right?"

"Yes. I've been working for him."

"And I am the first Nixie you have encountered."

Orla nodded, though it wasn't a question. She had learned in recent days that she was not the only citizen of Mithe in awe of Chusa and Faye. There were farmers and local merchants who drank at the inn and talked about the 'foreigners'. They accepted Ternell because he looked almost human but treated Chusa and Faye differently than one another.

"The Nixie's are known for making the best magical pieces in the world and I am sent every year to trade them in this city. They can protect the wearer, or make them more powerful. Here, let me show you."

She picked up an amulet and stepped closer to Orla. As Faye moved around the table, undoing the clasp, she looked up and their eyes met. Orla saw something familiar in her gaze and looked intently. Faye gasped, lowering her arms to her waist, the necklace forgotten in her hand. Faye inched closer to Orla and studied her eyes. She squinted in the sunlight and Orla's mind began to go blank.

All Orla could see or focus on was Faye. She began to hear a singing voice in her head, asking questions in a language she didn't understand. She wanted to answer, but didn't know how. The marketplace fell away and darkened in contrast with Faye's sharp, blue features.

Just as quickly as Faye had closed it in, Orla's mind expanded out again; drawn by Darragh's deep bellow. Orla reeled with the sudden flood of noise from the market and mid-day light.

"There you are!"

Orla stumbled back from Faye, looking around and gasping. *What was that?* She looked up at Faye with wide, questioning eyes, but Faye had returned to her normally composed self.

"I've been looking for you, Orla." Darragh towered above her as she caught her breath. He looked from woman to woman. "Everything all right?"

"It's fine. I was just showing our new friend some of my wares and she was overwhelmed by a particularly strong charm. I didn't realize you humans were so," she paused to choose her words, then looking to Orla, "fragile."

Darragh didn't seem to believe Faye but said nothing to contradict her.

"Orla, come to the inn. There's someone I'd like you to meet."

Orla straightened and eyed Faye once more before turning to leave. She didn't know what had just happened, but it was doubtful she'd visit Faye soon.

At the inn Darragh led Orla to a room in the back she'd not been in before. Large, heavy tapestries hung on the walls and an elaborately carved fireplace dominated one wall. This handsome room was obviously reserved for important guests, and as they entered a woman richly dressed in fine robe rose from a heavy chair to greet them.

"Orla, may I present the Gold Sage Maeve."

"P...pleased to meet you." Orla managed to get out. Maeve was tall and dominating, magnificent in her size and presence. A sage. *She's a wizard.* This woman was not a wizard on the street like the boy who lit the lamps, she was a woman of power and training. Her hair was dark with a few streaks of gray and her eyes a deep enough brown that in dark light they would appear completely black.

As Maeve stood, the ornate robes swept away and finely embroidered slippers poked from beneath them. She held a delicate and soft hand forward and Darragh introduced them.

"Maeve heads our wizard's enclave."

Orla was confused by the meeting and whipped her head to Darragh and back to Maeve, trying to understand why this woman was here at the inn waiting for her.

"Your friend told me an interesting story." Orla stopped looking about and settled her gaze on Maeve's, wide-eyed with her mouth agape.

"I...I didn't mean to...," she stammered.

"Please, sit." Maeve glided to the end of the table and Darragh moved off to the hearth and looked out the window. Orla stumbled as she moved to sit.

"Tell me about what happened."

"Well," Orla started slowly, "I was being attacked...I thought they would drop me and I'd be hurt. They were lifting me up, and... I was out of the reach of the others. I started screaming... the next I know I was on the ground and the imps were dead. Burnt."

"I see." Maeve didn't seem impressed and Orla feared what her judgment would mean. "You have no other recollection of the event then?"

"No. Nothing more than my hands tingling."

"May I see them?" Orla held her hands out to Maeve who turned each one over in with the occasional, "Hum."

What could she possibly be looking for? Orla could see mud caked under her nails and wanted to pull her hands away from Maeve; though she kept them still.

"It's not typical to see the new gifts in one as old as yourself, so you understand I question the legitimacy. Have their been any recent changes in your life? Does your body feel different at all?" Maeve leaned in, giving Orla little time to answer. Orla tried to keep her breath steady and stop herself from flushing.

"Have you been sick? You're too late for the second great change and too early for the third."

Maeve's volume increased, pressing Orla to answer her questions. Orla saw the last few months of her life flashing before her and didn't know what to say. So much of her life was hidden now, she's been trying to move past it and she didn't want to share it. Not with Darragh, who brought her here without her consent, or this overbearing woman who wanted to know far too much. After the uninvited attention of Faye earlier today and this inquisition, Orla had enough; she stood sharply.

"I'm sorry, but I must go." Maeve stood as well.

"Excuse me?" Maeve was not used to being spoken to this way and looked to Darragh, but Orla was nearly to the door and moving quickly. She ran through the tavern and out to the air with Faye's voice was ringing in her head in the strange language from before. Faye, Maeve, and Darragh together were breaking her concentration and the visions were threatening her again. She ran around the corner of the inn and leaned against the wall.

Taking a few long, deep breaths she closed her eyes, and began to gain control. Before she felt completely stable, she was shaken by the shoulders and opened her eyes.

"Why did you leave?" Darragh stood before her with a grip on her shoulders, almost in a rage. "Do you know who that was? Do you know how many favors I used to get you that meeting?" He paced and spoke out loud to himself. "Why am I even helping you? I don't even know you. I'm giving you work when you don't know how to fight and using my reputation with the most powerful wizard in our district. Why?" He stopped and paused for a moment, then turned to her.

"Why did you leave?" This time he waiting for a response.

"You didn't even ask me what I wanted!" Orla was not going to listen to him yell without returning with an outburst of her own. "You are correct, you don't know me. You do not know where I come from or why I am here, yet you bring some woman to examine me and my life? I know nothing of your wizards, how do I know you aren't taking advantage of me? Maybe I don't want to know what's happening. Maybe I don't want anyone else to know. The least you could have done was ask!"

Orla had exhausted her anger and they stood panting and fuming at one another waiting for them both to completely regain their calm.

"She wasn't asking about your personal life for her own amusement. Most wizards find their power as they become adults, and you would have reached maturity almost a decade ago. She was trying to understand why it would happen so late." Orla looked down and away.

"I didn't realize that..." she suddenly felt childish, "It's a very personal question... I wasn't ready for it." She paused to think and looked down at her hands. "You still had no right."

"An untrained wizard is dangerous. Not just to themselves, but to others around them and anyone you work with. If you lose your temper or you're attacked and can't control your power you could hurt someone."

Orla met his eyes and spoke with a serious tone, "But I'm not a wizard. I keep telling you; I'm not. It was a fluke. Maybe a real wizard was walking by and saw and wanted to help."

"Without saying anything?"

"It could happen." Orla was losing her resolve.

Darragh looked doubtful and Orla looked for any place to look but his face. He reached out and held her shoulder.

41

"The wizard enclave is not far from town. Please, let me take you there and you can see what Maeve teaches. She'll be able to tell if you really have magic in you and teach you to control it."

"I don't want to be a wizard. I'd know, wouldn't I?"

"You can't help what you are, Orla."

Orla set her feet and and lifted her chin, "I'm not comfortable with this."

"And if it means you're no longer in my employ?"

Orla was startled that he would make so drastic a comment. She hadn't expected that he would feel so strongly and he knew she didn't have a choice.

She wouldn't be able to survive in Mithe without a job and didn't want to be stuck working in the tavern. Her mind raced as she look for a solution, and finding none, she had little choice.

"Fine, I'll go."

"I want you to swear it. Tomorrow. I'll meet you here in the morning and take you myself."

"Fine, yes."

"You swear?"

"Yes. I swear."

Orla woke in the morning to another vivid dream of Cian and their humble home. It was different this time; a baby cried as she tried to nurse it. It wouldn't feed and the woman from her visions stood in the doorway scolding her in Faye's strange language. She woke to a pillow damp with tears. Wiping the moisture from her face, she rose and dressed with little attention to her hair matted in the trashing of her nightmare.

As she reached for the handle on the door of her room Orla remembered her promise. She had sworn to Darragh to visit the enclave and speak again with the Sage Maeve.

Orla didn't want to go. She'd given up everything in her life to find a place where no one knew her and no one knew about the visions. Now she discovered an even more terrifying ability and she was being asked to turn herself over to the most powerful person in the area. *What if it's a trap? What if that horrible woman is in charge and Darragh is working for her? I can't trust that woman.*

It was clear that not everyone believed as the villagers of her home did; that magic belonged to wadima and all other magic was dark and should be destroyed. She knew that these people saw beyond that, yet that broader sight didn't necessarily mean better intentions.

As she expected, Darragh was waiting at the bottom of the stairs in the tavern and Orla sighed at the sight of him. Mirna had porridge for them both and while eating Darragh took the opportunity to remind her that she'd sworn to go.

"I'm here, aren't I?" Is all Orla would say.

The day was overcast and Darragh led her through the city to the eastern gate. Beyond the gate the valley unfolded. Despite the haze it was a beautiful sight: green and fresh with a late spring shower. The valley floor was mostly grass or fields used to raise the crops that fed the city.

They passed low rock walls bordering fields of grains and early stalks of corn. Farmers working their fields took little notice of them, used to men and women on the roads. A fork split the road not far from town and they took the southern route on Darragh's lead.

They said little as they walked and Orla took in the expanse of valley, trying to occupy her mind. Change was becoming as regular to her as dressing in the morning and she didn't want to think about another one. She simultaneously wondered how the people in her village could be so removed from this world and if she'd ever know stability again.

As Orla began to sink into these deep thoughts the road came near to a tree line. The road wove on to the south and a small path split off to the east, barely noticeable to someone who wasn't looking for it. Orla was teased from her thoughts when Darragh veered from the road to the thin path. She looked doubtfully to him; but he ignored her and walked to the tree line.

They wound through tall, old evergreen trees for a few brief moments and then the woods gave way to a wide clearing. Darragh stepped to the side and paused to read Orla's face as she took in the open space. At the far end of the clearing the valley gave way to a sheer cliff face. Here a facade had been cut the entire length of the clearing, directly into the rock.

At either end stood great sentinels, statues of men as tall as the trees. They were armored, but instead of swords or spears they held staffs with ornately carved tops. Behind them was a recessed entryway, with pillars cut to look like trees and mimic the forest around them. After a moment Darragh smirked at Orla's expression and continued; she followed, anxious for more details.

Beyond the tree line the foot path turned to a wide lane spread with white gravel and bordered by sculptures of unfamiliar animals. Beyond the statues, the clearing gave way to gardens and a well kept lawn. In one garden near the path many different herbs were growing, some familiar to her and some not. Orla could identify simple remedy herbs like ginger and rosemary, used for nausea and upset stomach. It seemed odd to her that the garden of wizards would have such simple cures.

The garden and entrance were buzzing with activity. The youngest, no more than twelve or thirteen years, were weeding the garden under the supervision of their elders. A few in their later teens were reading on low benches books without names on the covers and others wrote in journals.

When they reached the rock face the gravel, grass and gardens ended at a cavernous entry way. Cut directly into the stone of the cliff, every bit was decorated with beautiful carvings. The pillars were all detailed to represent the bark of the surrounding trees. Orla craned her head to follow the pillars up to the ceiling with her eyes. At the tops of each pillar, branches were carved into a stone canopy.

Where the branches came together fire bowls hung down on chains for extra light. The bottom of the bowls were painted with birds, moths, and dragonflies. Benches, carved from the same stone, broke the entrance into sections. In one group of benches some students were showing off, conjuring fire, water, ice or smoke in their hands.

One young man noticed Orla watching and spun water from his hands. He made the water dance in a great spout. He twirled his fingers and it snaked above his head and twisted back in on itself in a fluid braid. He was watching her instead of paying attention to his great conjure and didn't notice when one of his classmates came behind with a blast of wind. The water spout froze instantly and then shattered down in a hail storm of ice chips.

The presence of so many young wizards eased Orla's greatest fears, though she still had reservations. The pillared arches gave way to a massive entrance with large carved wooden doors. They stood open and seemed too large to be moved by human force alone. Carved into the left door a male wizard held fire in his hand, the right a female with water. Around them every kind of creature to be imagined was carved with the wizards standing over them all.

46

Beyond the doors was a massive hall cut into the cliff-side, but instead of leading into darkness the ceiling gave a faint glow. Orla gaped up thinking, *How is it doing that?*

"It's enchanted," Darragh leaned over and whispered.

Orla was about to ask questions about how he knew, but as they stepped inside a man a few years younger than Orla came from a side door.

"Can I help you?"

"This woman is here to see Maeve."

The young man looked her over and passed a judgment that neither Darragh or Orla appreciated.

"Do you have an appointment? I do not recall seeing any visitors on her schedule this morning."

"No. I can assure you that Maeve will make time to see her. She takes a great interest in potential students."

"A potential student?" The man regarded her again. "Where are you from?"

"Northwest of here..." Orla began hesitantly. Before she could say more he interrupted her. Orla thought that Maeve taught her brand of manners as well as magic here.

"And when did you manifest?" Orla stammered and considered leaving when Darragh stepped in.

"I am an acquaintance of Maeve's and my companion will speak with her alone." Darragh removed a charm from around his neck and gave it to the young man. "Show her this and see what she says about her schedule."

The page left and Orla turned to Darragh.

"What was that?" She asked in a low voice.

"I have known Maeve a long time, and she knows my seal." Darragh realized how uncomfortable Orla was. "That boy is a fool. If he had any talent he would not be employed as Maeve's watch dog. Don't let him bother you."

Darragh looked up and seemed intent to say no more about it.

After a few moments the page returned, blushing, and asked Orla to follow him. She looked back to Darragh.

"Aren't you coming?"

"No. The halls of Eolas are for wizards alone. I'll remain here."

With this Orla faltered; without Darragh, if something went wrong it meant being without protection. She didn't trust Maeve or her rude students and the last thing she wanted was to be alone with them.

"You will be fine." Darragh said dismissively.

Orla had little choice and followed the page. From the main corridor they entered a small side door and wound up a spiral stair, also cut into the rock. They emerged into a small chamber and the page asked her to sit on one of the low benches. He passed through a door and a moment later returned.

"She'll see you now." Orla paused at the door while the page returned down the stair.

Orla was surprised to open the door to a flood of natural

light. The room was large and Orla began to wonder if the beds here were cut into stone as well. Wooden tables and book shelves lined each bit of wall not occupied by a door. Maeve was across the room removing protective eye wear and a canvas robe to protect her clothing; from which Orla recognized her husbands weaving, she looked away quickly before Maeve could catch her staring at it.

The ceiling of the room was domed oil-cloth with a staircase at the far end going out into direct sun. The haze from the morning had burned off to a beautiful late-spring day. Light flooded from above and it seemed Maeve's apartments broke through the top of the cliff.

"Ah, Orla. Welcome to my lab." Maeve moved to hang her robe and then stretched an arm to Orla. "Please, let's go to my office."

Orla followed Maeve through the lab and glanced at the tables. Glass vessels held liquids of different colors and consistency, jars of plants lined the far wall, and a mortar and pestle sat out on one table as she passed. She glanced in to see a dark yellow powder.

"It's just mustard seed, I'm afraid." Orla racked her brain for what magical purpose it could have. Maeve smiled, recognizing Orla's curious expression, "I like to cook."

Maeve moved through to her office and Orla obediently followed. Here the stone floor was covered in a beautiful rug and every bit of wall lined with with shelves. She scanned them, full of ornate boxes, unfamiliar gadgets, and volumes of books. One shelf alone held more books than Orla's entire village owned. In the center of the room was a high table with stools on either side. Maeve invited Orla to sit. They didn't speak for a few moments while Maeve regarded Orla, who shifted uncomfortably. Finally, Maeve folded her hands and leaned forward.

"What brings you to Eolas today? My impression yesterday was that you had no interest in us." Maeve spoke more gently than she'd done the day before.

"Darragh thought it best that I speak with you."

"I see... and what do you think?"

"I think Eolas is like nothing I've ever seen." Maeve smiled and Orla couldn't help but try and reconcile the two different people she seemed to be. The hard, pressing woman yesterday and the calm one before her now.

"I should apologize for the way I spoke yesterday. From your speech I gather that you're from the plateau people, is that right?"

Orla was surprised. It hadn't occurred to her that she had an accent or that it would give her away. It seemed so obvious now.

"Do not be alarmed. Knowing this tells me many things. Magic is rare in the plateau villages and even your medicine men, what is it you call them?"

"Wadima."

"Yes. Even your wadima can only work simple spells. I can understand you being so secretive. It's rare enough that we haven't sent anyone to look there in many years." Maeve paused and straightened on her stool.

"I realized after speaking with you that my questions may have seemed a bit forward."

With the mention of the questions Orla became uncomfortable. "Darragh explained them. I'm sorry if I was rude."

"Not at all. However, I would like to ask some more questions." She paused and when Orla did not object, continued. "Was the fire in the warehouse the first change you noticed?" Orla hesitated. She didn't expect this to be the first thing they would talk about. "There's no need to be afraid."

"I...see things...in my mind. I have a hard time controlling it sometimes."

Orla had expected Maeve to be surprised, but she didn't seem to be. Maeve continued her questions and Orla felt a growing sense of security.

"What do you see?"

"A woman, mostly. I don't know her...it's a little different every time." Orla paused, unsure what else to say and not wanting to talk about the demons. The more she talked about the visions the harder it became to control them.

Maeve paused for a few moments. In the silence she stood, but still said nothing. She walked to a cabinet on the far end of the room and removed a plain looking wooden box. She brought it back to the table and perched elegantly on her stool. Turning the box to Orla, she opened it to reveal three crystals.

"The first is a shard of amethyst, the second amber, the third onyx. Did you know that minerals affect visions?"

Orla looked up from the crystals to Maeve and noticed for the first time a sparkling purple charm like the one in the case, hung on an intricately linked chain: an amethyst.

"Yes," Maeve smiled into Orla's round-eyed expression, "my gift manifested with visions as well. My teacher found me at eleven barely able to stand and gave me this." She touched the necklace. "I could see the lives and deaths of every person I met as vividly as if they were happening in front of me.

"Imagine seeing your mother and your sisters and knowing exactly how each of them would expire. Over and over again, every time they entered a room. I was paralyzed with fear and no one in my family could understand why. I couldn't focus on day to day things at all.

"Few humans have this gift, but those that do must learn to control it. Amethyst helps the dampen the day to day visions. Amber will allow visions of good to be enhanced, and the Onyx will reveal evils." Maeve showed her each in turn.

"Why would anyone want to see more evil?"

"It's helpful to know what your enemies may be planning."

Orla thought she didn't have any enemies and wondered who would be so bold as to challenge Maeve.

Maeve stood and went to a tea tray at the side board. She waived her hand over the pot and brought it to the table. Orla still couldn't help but marvel at even these simple day to day uses of magic. As Maeve poured the tea she continued to speak.

"For a long time I couldn't resist the urge to wear an amber, wanting to see the joys of everyone around me. As with most young people in the first change, I wanted to experience everything the world could show me. So I did, through everyone I met. I could travel the world or read a book without spending a dime. I could have every lover they ever did and taste the best wine..." Maeve seemed to lose herself in thought for an instant.

"After a while I began to realize that knowing everything about the futures of others was impeding me from knowing them as people, so I wear the Amethyst most days now."

"So you can't see my life right now?"

"No. Not unless I remove it, or concentrate to see beyond it. I intentionally do not use that power anymore."

Orla wondered what she would do with such a power. She didn't even know if her visions were past or future, and they were mostly of people she'd never met. She'd occasionally see Cian in the village or other members of her family going about their chores and daily lives. Once she glimpsed Cian with a small child, but dismissed this as her wishful thinking.

Maeve was patient for a moment as Orla processed the new information and then gently interrupted her wandering thoughts.

"Tell me about when the visions started."

Orla hesitated. This was not a story she wanted to tell and and hadn't anticipated being asked for it. She watched her hands working one another on her lap.

"Not more than six moon cycles ago I was with child." She could feel a lump rising in her throat and paused to let it pass. "I was very far along. It was nearly my term and I became ill. One of the merchants who had traded with my husband had brought an early winter flu to our village and I caught it."

A tear rose to her eye and she quickly wiped it away before it would fall. Maeve said nothing and watched her face.

"I remember very little of what happened and my husband refuses to talk about it. What I do know is that I babbled in a language that no one in my village knew... an old woman claimed to have heard it before. When I asked her about it later she told me to forget she'd said anything.

"The wadima worried that the fever would hurt my baby and forced a tincture to induce contractions. I vomited all through the labor and had a high fever. They were able to save me," Orla gasped, but forced herself to continue, "the baby died before it could take it's first breath." Orla looked down and away. She'd never said these things aloud before, though she'd relived them in countless nightmares. The sentences were heavy in her throat.

"The baby was sick... there was nothing anyone could do. As I regained my strength the visions started and I was nearly driven mad." Orla chuckled awkwardly as she wiped the tears from her face. "I thought I *had* lost my mind. I couldn't get out of bed for weeks. My husband thought he'd lost both wife and daughter.

"Eventually, I was strong enough to hold the visions to the

back of my mind. I could do simple tasks, but there were times when I was overwhelmed. At the start of the last moon cycle I fled. I was afraid that they would think the bad birth had filled me with an evil spirit and burn me."

Maeve watched her tea while Orla dried her eyes and waited for her breathing to relax.

"It's very odd, your story." Maeve said.

"Yes. Darragh said that human wizard only get their gifts during the second great change of life."

"It's true. I've never met a human who didn't; until now."

"Does that mean there's something wrong with me?"

"Not necessarily. I'd like to look into it further; in the mean time, I'd also like to ask you to study here at Eolas." Orla looked up to meet her gaze.

"You really think I belong here?"

"You'll be starting with student's much younger than you, though it wouldn't be the first time that's happened."

Until now, Orla had been staying in Mithe out of convenience and a lack of anywhere else to go. She wanted to trust Maeve, to believe that this woman sincerely desired to help, and to build a stable place for herself. More than that, Orla wanted to know that she wasn't insane and that her powers were a gift and not a curse.

"I'll accept your offer, though only if I can continue to live in Mithe. I wouldn't feel right here."

"I think that can be arranged for. I also think you should

know that your gifts are considerable. Most of the students that have been here for years can not do what you did in the warehouse."

"Really? But there was a boy in the entrance playing with water. It was incredible. I can't do what he can do..."

"Yes, that must have been Jayna." Maeve's face bloomed into a coy smile. "He likes to show off. He is a master of the water elements at only twenty, but is behind with the other elements. Jayna came here very young, only ten years old. He has a natural affinity for water and almost drowned his village before we found him. He's been studying a long time, don't measure yourself against him."

"Even if I don't; I couldn't do what I did to the imps again."

"You'll find that different people have different gifts and everyone works at different speeds. Some here are children of wizards and know all the herbs and remedies before they arrive. Others, like yourself, take years before an enclave discovers them or they find us. The only scale that matters is you against your own potential.

"Here, put this on." Maeve lifted the amethyst crystal from the box and a long, silver chain snaked below it.

"That must be very expensive. I can not..."

"Nonsense. We can't have you distracted in your classes by visions you can't control. Think of it as a loan."

"I don't have any money... and I'd like to continue working for Darragh..."

"Do not concern yourself with payment. I'm sure we can work out a schedule for you to continue working if that's your preference."

Maeve was dangling the crystal from it's chain and Orla reached out her hand to take it; from the moment it touched her palm a cool, easy calm spread out from the center of her hand. As it eased its way up her arm she took the necklace in both hands, lifted the chain over her head and let the amulet settle onto her chest. Closing her eyes, she felt her jaw unclench for the first time in months. Her mind was silent. Peaceful. She was suddenly very tired, lost for a few moments in the blanket of calm.

Opening her eyes, Orla looked into Maeve's motherly expression. Orla was drawn in, so different from her first impressions of the sage.

"You should get back to Mithe, I'm sure you have preparations to make. I'll expect you to be here in three days to start your lessons."

Orla stood, thanked Maeve, and started toward the door while Maeve moved toward one of her many bookshelves. Orla paused before reaching the door and turned.

"Mistress?"

"Yes?"

Orla paused from embarrassment and wondered if what she had to say would cost her this new opportunity. She glanced to the many books on Maeve's shelves.

"Few people in my village ever learn to read. I can work

numbers and basic mathematics...b...but not letters." Orla's ears were burning red and she was thankful her hair was down to cover her complexion. Here eyes were down and she couldn't see Maeve's smile.

"We have all types here. I'll assign a tutor and we can teach you."

"Thank you." As Orla turned to go she glanced around the shelves again, eager to be able to read them herself, and noticed Maeve pull a small book from the shelf in front of her. It was a beautiful shade of robin's egg blue with silver edged pages. Orla felt pulled by the book, not only wanting to read it, but to just hold it in her hands. She didn't want to pry, so she didn't ask about it; but the book stuck in her mind.

Chapter Five

With the visions no longer haunting her and her time split between working for Darragh and her studies at Eolas, Orla felt the spring grow quickly into summer.

With the new season Mithe also grew with a steady influx of merchants and travelers. Mirna kept a garden just outside the city walls and in the late afternoons Orla would joined her in weeding and planting; she was quickly becoming the closest thing Orla had to a friend here. Orla had taken a permanent room in a boarding house near the inn to keep close to the people she was already comfortable with. She still had breakfast with Mirna and when business with Darragh was slow, she would waitress in the tavern.

Mirna was single and gossiped every day about the men in Mithe, who was courting whom and why it was so incendiary.

Like the weeding, Orla felt this idle chatter kept her grounded. Like her cousins back home, Mirna was more of a talker than a listener and Orla didn't mind.

Her studies were going very well. Orla was learning how to read and write, how to work spells and rituals, and how to cast simple enchantments. She was also learning the history of wizards and where to find information when doing research. Researching was hard with her limited reading, though many at the school were pleased to help her. Only a few resented her age and connection to Maeve, to which Orla was oblivious.

Her days at Eolas were split between practical lessons, tutoring, and lectures. Some sunny days the classes would meet out in the entry way and try to focus on the speaker instead of on the dappled sunlight of the trees. Today was one of those days.

The lecturer was a traveler from the far south named Vibraz who had arrived at Eolas only a few days before. Orla hadn't met him, but heard the younger girls talking about him; they were right, he was good looking but Orla found him too arrogant to be attractive. He wore his hair long and wild, and dressed in pants with a leather vest that showed his tan chest. One of the other students pointed out in a book that this was the traditional dress of the southern people, but Orla wasn't impressed.

He'd come to study with Maeve and she required more experienced students to instruct the newer pupils. He was assigned to teach those who came from non-wizard backgrounds the general knowledge they would need. He strutted back and forth, and while he talked he flipped his hair out of habit. Orla tried to concentrate on his lesson, but found herself counting hair flips instead.

"Wizards are divided by two categories: one is the class of magic you practice and the other is your rank." *Flip* "The magical classes are: Suspenders, who levitate objects; Aesculpians, who have the ability to heal and aid others medically..." a cricket was chirping in the corner and Orla began to drift from the self-important drone of Vibraz's lecture to follow the sound. She snapped herself back, determined to learn everything she could.

"...and Elementalists, who can manipulate the four natural elements.

"Some of you will have your path chosen for you by the nature of your talents; others will be able to chose a path. I," *flip,* "am an earth elementalist." To demonstrate this, he flipped his wrist and a block of stone came free from the cliff wall behind him. He hovered it over his head and spun it like a globe while the girls sitting next to Orla gasped with infatuated awe. Without looking up or back, he twisted his shapely hand and the stone returned to its original place without a crack in the cliff. Many students applauded, though Orla was too focused on her own thoughts. *I'm an elementalist, and I can do more than just pull a stone from a wall.*

Vibraz had begun talking again and Orla wrestled herself from rolling the words around in her mind to pay attention.

"The class of your magic is the type your able to do, while rank is given based on your knowledge and control. The ranks are named based on the preciousness of metals. As I'm sure you know, Maeve is a Gold, one of the highest ranks. I" *flip* "am Iron." The infatuated girls cooed and he scanned the class, "I'm sure if you're here your copper."

A copper elementalist. Everyone starts somewhere.

"If a wizard is able to reach Iron in every class they are known to other wizards as a Sage. It's a great honor and there are only seven Sages in the known world." *Flip* "Advanced wizards will comb the world to find Sages to study with and many only accept the best to personally tutor." With this Vibraz gave a great hair *flip* and Orla took it to imply that he was one of the best because he was studying with Maeve.

Another of the general classes at Eolas was intended to teach the building blocks necessary to control the elements and manipulate everyday matter. After only a few weeks of study Orla could light a fire on the ground an arms length in front of her. A few weeks after that she could conjure a ball of water or fire the size of her first and lift it from the ground. If she had been paying attention she would have realized that the students around her could barely make a spark.

Due to her quick studies Maeve removed her from the class and assigned her a tutor, Jayna, the wizard who had shown off her first time at Eolas.

Jayna lived at the enclave and, though he was a few years

younger than Orla, he had seen much more of the world. He described to her in great detail the deserts to the south and great magical beasts that lived in the mountains on the far side of the world. Orla had a hard time telling the difference between what was real and what was made up; and the pranks he was fond of playing didn't help her believe him. Every time she was sure he'd created the creature he described she would find in referenced in one of the books she was learning to read.

Orla was captivated by her ever-expanding world enough to distract her from what she had left behind. She discovered there were even more races and in her reading found creatures that made Chusa seem meek as a lamb.

A few days each week Darragh and Ternell had work for Orla. It gave her an opportunity to hone her new found skills and earn extra gold for school, as well as to help pay for any damage caused with an occasional back-fired spell.

One afternoon in late summer, Jayna met Orla on the banks of the river halfway between Mithe and Eolas. In the last few weeks it rained very little and Maeve had been asked by the farmers to help sustain their crops until a natural solution returned. Jayna, entrusted with the job, wanted to use this as a teaching opportunity.

Jayna was tall and lanky, with sandy-brown hair and a

smile that took up half his face. The first time Orla saw him laugh she thought his cheeks were elastic because they seemed to expand out beyond the edges of the rest of his face. His hair was always messy, but the rest of him kept clean as he spent most of his time working with water.

Jayna was walking on a retaining wall by the river and telling Orla about the practical day-to-day uses of magic that help to keep the town going; specifically about helping with crops.

"I know you haven't worked on anything this large yet, but I'm sure you can handle it." He jumped down from the wall and landed two steps in front of Orla.

"We're here!" He said, and pointed across the river to a small farm. The fields were dry and even from this distance Orla could tell that the plants were withered. She wondered aloud why the farmers didn't call Maeve before.

"We aren't a charity, Orla. Maeve is generous, but doesn't give the services of her students for free. Most of the magic you see around Mithe is paid for and if the student's can't afford to study at Eolas she wont turn them away. She trades their work to the town and the farmers and they help keep us all in business."

"Oh." Orla hadn't thought much about how to make a living as a wizard; though now that Jayna pointed it out it seemed obvious.

"Alright. Let's get to work."

Jayna had her close her eyes and let her breathing fall to a deep rhythm. She'd been taught early in her time at Eolas that control of magic comes from concentration and focus and the breathing increased her control. He talked her through the mediation and concentration exercises they had been practicing. She pulled air deep in her chest through her nose and blew it out her mouth. In her mind she saw the pieces that made up the water and how to control them.

Jayna's voice melded in with her meditation. "Now, levitate the water. Open your eyes to see only the water you want to move."

Orla opened her eyes and could feel the river as an extension of herself. It pulsed with the beat of her heart and breath and she could feel the movement of each particle sweeping past one another. From this connection she lifted a ball of water and swept it out over the first field. The tiny particles danced against one another inside the ball and she let little bits escape to rain down on the field. A huge smile spread across her face and a larger drop than she intended crashed down.

"Careful..." Jayna coached gently, "keep your focus."

She reinforced the boundaries of the ball with her mind and moved it out over the next bit of field. She let the rain fall from her sphere-cloud and repeated the same process until each field was moist and the plants began to straighten.

"Very good." Jayna had an edge of excitement in his voice. "Before you start celebrating ease it back to the river. No good to flood out the crops that you're trying to save." Orla swept the water back above the river. "Ok. Let go."

Orla dropped the remaining water back into the river with a laugh and a shout. It slammed with a splash into the normally tranquil waters below and small waves sloshed up over the banks. The thirsty fields didn't mind and Orla and Jayna didn't notice. She was dancing and he was laughing.

"Thank you!" she yelled and leapt to hug him. He wrapped his arms around her and then she froze. She realized that the only man other than her immediate family to touch her this was was her husband. She let go quickly and pulled away, leaving Jayna confused and startled.

"Thank you for the lesson." She looked awkwardly from the water to the stone wall and started walking back toward the path, unsure what to say. Jayna followed after her.

"Of course. You're a great student. I've never seen anyone learn so fast." The moment had passed while they made their way back to Mithe, Jayna steered the conversation back to spellwork.

"You can use that same technique on any matter, not just elements you can control. You've got the basics of lightweight levitation. Now we'll want to focus on practicing and maintaining your concentration. The longer you can sustain it the more effective you'll be for long-term use. How is your conjuring coming."

"Fair. I can conjure small amounts of water and fire and control them, but I can't consistently get a good breeze or control anything other than the four natural elements."

"They can be very hard for an elementalist, I still have trouble the caustics. Once you move to more advanced elementalism you wont really need those other skills."

They chatted idly and walked while the sun lowered in the

66

hills. They reached Mithe, said good bye, and Orla headed to the tavern to join Mirna, Ternell and Lorcian for dinner.

Outside in the square Orla could hear an unusually large crowd in the tavern. While she knew Mirna could use her help, the spell in the fields had exhausted her and she was looking forward to an early, full night of sleep. Orla was trading simple magic tasks in the boarding house for a down cover on her mattress. She'd been indulging in the luxury of living in town and all the simple pleasures she could now afford.

Opening the door to the tavern, Orla was greeted with a wave of noise and laughter. Traders was staying at the inn and they filled the tavern with conversation. Most travelers stayed at the camp outside Mithe, though Orla overheard the men say they had been out for a long time and the promise of a hot meal cooked by someone else was too strong a lure.

Her dinner companions usually met at a table Mirna kept for them near the hearth, though it was empty when Orla arrived. Mirna only had a moment to pause and explain that Darragh, Ternell, and Lorcian had all left messages that they would see Orla tomorrow. She would be eating alone tonight, but didn't mind.

Now that the visions were under control and she no longer needed a distraction, being alone was sometimes nice. She liked to let her mind wander, especially with all she'd recently learned, and tonight she paused to consider what it meant to have had her arms around Jayna today.

Orla's train of thought was sharply interrupted, cut through by a familiar voice.

"Cian's an excellent weaver, don't get me wrong, but I know I'll be asked about that satin his wife used to make. Without her work I'll be taking a loss this year."

"What happened to her? She die?"

"No one's sure. They say she just vanished out of her bed one night. Husband woke and she was gone. They think she either ran away or was kidnapped when she went out to relieve herself."

"Strange... there aren't many places to hide up there. And why just take a woman like that?"

"The old woman in their village raved for awhile about witchcraft; but you know how those outer villages are...they'll believe anything."

Orla could barely breathe and her mouth had gone dry. Her. They were talking about her.

She recognized the trader, one of their largest customers who carried a fine berry wine from the eastern continent; he always saved a bottle for her. He'd liked to tell her about the far off places her fabrics went and the wealthy people who requested them. Orla would take special orders from him for colors and designs and have them ready when he made his return from the western coast in the fall. He would recognize her if he saw her.

Orla bent her head and hid her face and her blood pounded in her ears. *What do I do?*

She breathed carefully, as Jayna and Maeve had taught her, to help control her emotions. *Out of control emotions can lead to out of control magic.* Her pulse slowing and her mind ran through what she had learned, but nothing seemed to help. She'd heard about people who could disguise themselves, but didn't know how to do it; and fire or water wasn't going to help.

She got up from the table and headed for the back door to Mirna's courtyard with her shrine to Danu. There was no gate and little to stand on. Here eyes fell on the shrine and she felt the bite of blasphemy just below her ribs. Orla stepped up on the alter, next to the statue of the earth goddess, and could just reach the top of the fence. With all her energy she pulled herself up and over the top, careful not to kick the statue. *So much for the mighty wizard.*

After landing on the other side, she rounded the building and into the kitchen. Mirna came in with a gasp.

"Weren't you just out there?" she exclaimed

"There are some people I care to avoid. Here's the money for my meal. I'm sorry to slip out when you're so busy."

Mirna waved with a smile and shook her head, not pretending to understand what might have gotten into her friend. Orla turned and left for the boarding house, ready to sleep after a full day of excitement.

Safely back in her room, Orla changed into her night shirt; but something was bothering her. She'd walked into the inn and looked right at the table; she even smiled at a few of the men and said hello to the regulars from the town. The traders must have seen her, but none of them said anything.

She absentmindedly started to brush her hair out and conjured a light in the oil lantern. A glimpse of her reflection in the window and she thought: *That's why he didn't recognize me.*

Orla stared at herself, seeing what the merchant saw. Not the woman from a small village in Ardlan, but a town wizard. She wore finer clothes and the crystal on a fine chain around her neck with her hair longer than she'd ever kept it while weaving fabrics. Her face was leaner and more serious than it was in her simple village life and she'd lost the extra weight she used to carry. Before her was the Copper Elementalist Orla, not the weaver's wife. A woman who could write her name and almost read and manipulate water and fire. She couldn't help but smile with a bit of pride.

When she'd first arrived in Mithe, Orla had told herself she'd only stay a short time and as she approached the end of summer she wondered if it was wise to stay. She'd been distracted by all that had happened. Though she knew she could protect herself and she was safe from the elders of her village she didn't want to return to her former life. It was only a matter of time before an acquaintance of her husband recognized her.

Poor Cian. Orla thought, turning from the window and snuffing the light. She settled into bed in the sudden darkness and missed the weight of a man next to her. She thought of the old bed they had shared and wished he could lie on the soft down next to her, that she could share with him what her gifts had brought her, to see what she had become and feel proud like she did. For the first time she was thinking about home without crying. She liked her new life, even if she missed her husband. She drifted to sleep with him in her minds eye.

Chapter Six

Heat. It was all she could feel as it singed her hair and throat. Incredible heat that was pulled into her lungs with every rough, rattling breath and it pulled her to consciousness. A flare up burned so close she could feel it scorching her eyebrows. Orla coughed and tried to orient herself in the smoke.

A clearing? she thought, *How did I get here?*

Through the haze Orla could see tall, old trees with their leaves wilting and the tips of the long, wide branches were sizzling and popping with heat. The ground was packed sod with a thick cover of grass and the small flowers near her ankles were browning; all around her the clearing burned.

Concentrate. She tried to control her breathing but gagged with every throat full of smoke. Her mind was clouded and disoriented and, in the panic, her magic failed. She couldn't focus long enough to conjure water, and even if she could she wasn't powerful enough to stop this fire. A pang of helplessness knotted her stomach.

Orla swung her head around and desperately searched for a way to escape. Not far from her, just inside the tree line, was a large rock with a split wide enough to grip in and a flat spot near the top to perch on. If she could scramble up above the smoke it might be high enough for fresh air, and maybe she could survive long enough for the fire to burn out.

She struggled and scrapped her arms and legs on the rock. Her feet felt heavier than normal and the choking smoke made the exertion even harder. Orla was not used to climbing and the crack wasn't as much help as she had hoped.

In her desperation she summoned the strength to pull up the last few feet, but while she was climbing the dry brush around the base had caught in a mighty flare. Flames heated the rock from below and smoke curled up around her. Orla could feel it biting in her lungs and throat and she fell to her knees.

The smoke was clouding her mind and the heat was agony. She couldn't help but scream with pain; but when she did it sounded odd. The scream sounded too far away to be her own, and it was higher and gruffer than her own voice.

Orla focused on the screaming and, when she did, it began to separate into two distinct voices: one her own, and another higher-pitched wailing. The breathing was the same, but the screams were different. Orla focused harder on the screaming.

Orla woke gasping and heaved to breathe in the relief of fresh air. She struggled to stand, tripping on the bedding and pulling the mattress half onto the floor. Her eyes were wide and her head pounding. She could see an unfamiliar creature behind her eyes, screaming in the same terrible high-pitched growl she heard in the dream. The vision was strong and clear and she was watching the creature she had been in the dream.

Fighting for control, Orla concentrated on her breathing and untangled herself from the knotted mass of blankets while little puffs of down floated to the ground. As she stood something fell to the floor with a knock; it was the amethyst charm.

Anxious to block the unwelcome howling from her mind, Orla quickly snatched it up. With a tight fist she gripped it and the screams began to fade.

She checked the clasp and other bits of metal work and found no damage. It hadn't broken and fallen off, but she hadn't removed it either. It was long enough to fit over her head, but she was doubtful it could have come lose on its own.

It took a while for Orla to relax again, but once settled in, she slept through the rest of the night.

The next few days were uneventful. The horrid dream of the burning creature faded in the warm summer days and bright sun. Darragh and Ternell asked her to stay close, but didn't say much about why and didn't have any work for her. Orla took the extra time to enjoy a few luxuries: she could eat a great variety of foods, try different ales and wines, but by far her favorite was sleeping in.

Before coming to Mithe, every day began early with chores like waking to draw water and stoke the fire. In the good fortune of summer she could buy bread from the neighbor, but in the winter they conserved their resources so she added making it to her list of things to be done early. She would spend the mornings foraging, doing simple repairs on their cottage or mending clothing. In the afternoons she would weave with Cian.

Now, dawn would break and she could stay in bed a while longer. With Darragh and Ternell away she could lay there and enjoy the warm comfort of her boarding house. She listened to the mistress prepare the morning meal and the merchants opening shops on the street. Sometimes she thought of home and sometimes just rolled her head back to lie in the sun of her east facing window.

At first she felt decadent and guilty, her habit meant that someone else was drawing her water and keeping the fires burning. Later she realized that the gold she paid for their service kept them in their homes and she felt better. With that bit of rationale she was free again to sleep through the dawn and wake at her leisure.

A few days a week Orla attended class at Eolas, where she

was getting more comfortable visiting and spending time. She read simple things and her time was improving at conjuring water and freezing it.

The more advanced students could do this trick so fast that non-magical people assumed they could conjure ice itself. Early in her studies Orla thought this as well, until she began to learn the basics of the trick: to conjure water and freeze it the moment it materializes. Jayna and his friends gave her a few tips, the best of which was to see the whole process before she began. To not think of it as steps, but as one fluid motion.

She spent her remaining time practicing. With her literacy too low to study books, and little else to do, she sat by the river levitating water, turning it to ice, and letting it drop back in. She also practiced her fire conjuration, though was careful to do it above the middle of the river where it would do little damage if she lost control. This is where Darragh found her one afternoon, a creek of water seeming to appear from nowhere and flow down to join the river.

"Very nice." He called from up the hill, "I'm pleased."

Orla blushed a little; another frequent reaction she was learning to control. "Thank you. It's not much."

"It's significant. A few months ago you couldn't look up from your shoes long enough not to bump into anything and now you're mastering the elements. I'd say that's a lot." Orla was unsure what to say with Darragh standing over her, smiling and paying complements. She shaded her eyes from the sun to look at him. "Ternell and Lorcian are waiting at Mirna's tavern for me. If you're not to busy," He gestured to the water, "you should join us."

"Of course." Orla said with a little too much enthusiasm. The water splashed back into the river and she scrambled to join him above the bank. Darragh wasn't normally so formal. He typically waited to meet her at breakfast and gave her work. *What's so urgent that he'd come and find me?*

Orla followed Darragh back to the tavern, unsure if she should ask questions. He broke the silence by asking about her magical studies and reading. She guessed that it was intended to distract her, but it didn't work.

Darragh led the way through the door of the tavern. Afternoon sun was streaming in through the front windows and Orla was surprised not to see Ternell and Lorcian inside. Darragh kept striding across the room and she hurried to follow him, catching up as he entered the same grand room where he'd introduced her to Maeve.

Lorcian and Ternell waited inside with none of their usual chatter. They'd been summoned with the same serious tone and left to wait and wonder while Darragh fetched Orla. She was surprised to find Chusa among them as well, sitting imposingly in a carved, wide-seated chair, twice as large as Lorcian and Ternell's normal tavern chairs.

Chusa alone was drinking; a blood wine that Mirna carried for some of the non-human guests. Orla had never tried it and wasn't sure she ever would. He tried to joke with her as she entered.

"Little wizard," He called out to her with the nickname he'd given her since she started at Eolas. "How are you?"

"I'm well. Thank you, Chusa." Only recently had Orla been able to address the massive drasta without her voice wavering. She normally only saw him in the square and had never seen him indoors before. He seemed to fill one side of the large table all himself. He hadn't worked with Darragh and Ternell, at least not in the time that Orla was here. So she was left to wonder, *What is he doing here?*

Darragh stood at the end of the table and Orla sat quickly next to Ternell.

"I apologize for the secrecy. I've been asked to do my best to keep from adding to rumors and I intend to comply. I'm sure you've heard by now the stories coming from the merchants."

Orla hadn't. Since the night she was nearly recognized she had tried to avoid them. Darragh must have read her blank expression and his voice changed as he deviated from his planned speech.

"There are rumors about fires in the forest to the east, Orla. Merchants are saying they are started magically and, after they catch, whole sections of the forest are destroyed." He paused for a moment as if about to find his place and then turned back to her again. "If you're serious about working with us you might want to

78

start talking to people more."

Orla lowered her head a little, not wanting this kind of attention. She didn't want the others to look too closely at who she was speaking to and who she was avoiding. Fortunately, Darragh continued.

"The merchant guilds of Mithe and Naynor and the tribes of Irwu are all threatened by the fires. They have pooled their resources and asked Ternell and I to investigate the cause." He'd reached the end of his prepared introduction and waited. There was silence for a few moments and even Chusa was still. Then it seemed he couldn't help himself.

"Well. Any ideas?" Chusa said with a toothy, sarcastic half smile.

"I have a few, though none with any real grounding. The tribesmen of Irwu believe it's a foul spirit they angered somehow. Obviously, I'm not entertaining that too seriously. Mithe's elders are unsure..."

"And what about Naynor?" Chusa cocked his head up and looked over his snout to Darragh. Orla didn't understand why, but she could feel the anger in his voice. He was being defensive and Darragh seemed to know he was in careful territory.

"They are concerned... that it might be attacks by drasta." He said this last bit very quickly, as if speeding through it could draw less attention to it.

"WHAT?" Chusa roared, his is words accompanied by a rumble in his chest like nothing Orla had heard come from something so nearly human. Steam was curling up from the

79

nostrils at the end of his snout-like face. "How dare you imply..."
Darragh was unaffected and cut him off with a raise of his voice.

"I am implying nothing." Orla was caught in the intensity of
Darragh's gaze. He did not waiver before Chusa's aggression and
held his ground with both feet planted. "I am answering your
question... and the answer is why you are here." Darragh held
Chusa's gaze for an instant and then began to relax. Amazingly,
Chusa followed this lead in body language and the tension in the
room started to unravel.

"I thought you would appreciate an opportunity to prove
them wrong and build some trust for your people." Darragh's
voice was a crafted blend of control and ease. Chusa seemed
appeased for the moment and sat back in his chair.

"I think they're all wrong." Darragh continued, glancing to
Chusa. "I think there's something else going on and we're going to
find it and all be well rewarded for it. Now," Darragh sat among
them, pulled a scroll from his bag, and unfurled it on the table
between them. Despite herself, Orla interrupted and reached her
fingers toward the scroll.

"Is this a map of the world?"

Darragh smiled.

"No. This is just our half of the world," He glanced around
the table and, sensing no objections, continued with a geography
lesson. "Here we are in the hills of Nanir, just to the east of the
plateau. To the west of them are the inland sea and beyond the
mountains in the north west. The hills continue for some time,
and overlap with the beginnings of the great forest of Irwu to our

east. Many days journey from here, on the other side of the forest, is the city of Naynor on the coast to the south east. This road through the forest is the main passage, and what we are going to protect.

"South of the forest and hills are plains and beyond them a small desert. There are two other great continents, and one small one far to the south where Ternell is from," at this Ternell gave a little nod and a smile, "and a few island here and there."

Orla gazed down at the map trying to take it all in. Darragh began again, though she only caught every few phrases.

"Not knowing what we'll find means I'm unsure what to bring. I trust each of you and that's why I'm asking you to come with me. I'll lead us to the main Irwu village of Ni'Ca. There we'll gather information and I know a guide who is reliable and doesn't give into the superstitions of most of his people. I'd like to leave in the morning and it will be two days travel to Ni'Ca by horse." They all sat for a moment and then Chusa nodded broadly.

"I'm sorry I doubted you." He said with a laugh. "I'll come. Why not?"

Lorcian was next to agree and Orla looked up to Darragh and nodded. She waited for the others to move to the tavern and stepped behind Darragh.

"I'd like to speak with you."

"Yes?" He stepped back into the room, seemingly unaffected by the concern on Orla's face.

"I don't think I'm ready." Orla said it to her hands, and

when Darragh didn't respond she looked and could read on his face that he wasn't taking her seriously. "I mean it. I barely know how to work simple spells and I don't know how any of them could be used to help you or the others." The feeling of helplessness from her dream began to fill her again, like smoke in her lungs.

"I wouldn't ask you if I didn't think you could be useful-"

"And what if I'm not and someone gets hurt trying to protect me?"

"I've spoken with Maeve." Darragh was calm and assuring. Orla wondered how this could be the same leader that stood up to Chusa so recently. "We both agreed that it's time for you to start testing your powers. You can't use daggers and spears forever, that's not what wizards do, and you wont be of nearly as much use to me with a little knife." Orla was still nervous, but had decided to trust Darragh and Maeve.

"Ok. I'll come. But I'm sure there are things I need that I don't have." Darragh chuckled.

"I think we can help you with that." He rested his hand on her shoulder and steered her into the tavern where the others already had ales for themselves with two more waiting for them. Darragh turned to Lorcian.

"I hope you aren't doing anything this afternoon. I have a job for you."

 chapter seven

The afternoon of crisscrossing the squares of Mithe calmed some of Orla's anxiety. She enjoyed picking out her horse to rent, buying a bed roll, rope, a belt and pouches for small items, a tinderbox, rations, a small knife, chalk, water flask (though this felt odd for a wizard who could make water), whistle, mirror, and pack to hold it all.

As a gift to herself, Orla bough a beautiful deep blue traveling cloak from Faye; she was sure to bring Lorcian to keep her safe from any of Faye's tricks. It was a cloak of resting, that helped the wearer keep weariness at bay on long journeys. At the neck was a fine clasp plated in silver and the hood and hem were trimmed in an ivy vine of gray threaded embroidery.

Faye explained that only Nixie women were magical and the embroidery was how the magic was worked into a garment; for armor and other metal goods it was in the engraving. She continued to explain that as Orla wore it it would become more and more attached to her and be increasingly more affective.

After the shopping Orla returned to her room with the bundles and packages. Now alone with time to think Orla felt guilty about spending that much when she didn't need to. She thought of the good that she could do in her village with that kind of money, but quickly pushed the thought from her mind. *They would never understand who you are now. It was their close-mindedness that drove you from home and you deserve this for surviving.*

Orla had placed the cloak on top of her pack across the room. She stared at it from the edge of her bed, the clasp catching the light. She thought about all she'd learned and all she'd left. She let herself feel the fear of the trip to the Irwu forest and the doubt that she was not ready.

She crossed the room, lifted the cloak, and brought it around her shoulders. She immediately felt the boon, as if she'd just woken from a much-needed nap. She smiled at the fine fabric and hugged it around her. Faye hadn't even needed to hem it, as if the cloak had been made for her. Orla decided to wear it out to the tavern and join Mirna for dinner.

A meal and a conversation with Mirna helped Orla to feel better. With the warm weather most travelers were camping outside the city and the tavern wasn't busy. While Mirna's hired servants handled the kitchen she sat and talked with Orla, drinking imported berry wine and eating summer squash stew.

Orla relaxed and looked across the table at her friend; thankful for someone to talk to who wanted nothing in return but her companionship.

Though Darragh had asked them not to discuss it, Orla knew she could trust Mirna. She wasn't sure where to start and tried to tell her about the fires and the Irwu; but Mirna interrupted her, leaning in close.

"Ternell was drunk most of tha afternoon. I kno wher' you'r' goin'."

"You do?" Orla was surprised and relieved. Now she didn't have to try and tell Mirna herself. "I don't think I can do it."

"Wha'? Go with 'um? Sure ya' can."

"No, I can't." Orla gazed around the tavern, "What if something bad happens and it's my fault?"

"Darragh's a good lead'r. He wouldn' take ya if he didn' know fa' sure that ya' were ready." Mirna smiled at Orla, "Ya've changed a lot since ya got here. I like that ya're wearing ya hair longer, it looks good tha way." *Why's she changing the subject? Doesn't she think I can do it?*

Reaching under her chair, Mirna pulled out a small package and put it on the table. "I got ya somethin' after Ternell left. I thought ya might need it on the road." Orla laughed a little, embarrassed.

"Aren't you going to open it?" Mirna asked.

Orla unwrapped the simple fabric and inside was a small half dome cage and a little polished stick. The cage was made of a think wire woven and spun around itself and the stick was hard wood with a decorative carving at one end.

"It's ta keep your hair up while ya ride... and I thau't it's pretty."

It had been a long time since Orla had received a present from a friend. A few months ago she would have doubted that she'd ever have a real friend again and Orla smiled broadly across the table at Mirna.

"Ya're goin' to be fine. I'll see ya in a few weeks, and keep ma nephew out'ta trouble."

Orla slept on a full stomach and woke slowly the next day. She didn't want to get out of her comfortable bed. She looked through the dirty window and watched the birds swoop through the sky above Mithe. *It's going to be a long day.*

chapter Eight

By the time Orla dressed and met the others their packs were secured on their horses. They teased her for sleeping in, but it was obviously in good fun. Orla could feel their excitement about embarking on the adventure and in turn she wondered if they could feel her doubt.

Ternell showed Orla how to secure her pack to a light gray horse she chose the day before. The stable master called her "Freidya" and said she was the most gentle horse he had.

"It means peace in my language." Ternell said as he secured the last lash to the saddle. "This will be a good horse for you."

The riding wasn't easy; Orla had only ridden a horse for fun, never for travel. After a few hours her hips hurt and her back was sore. Not wanting the men to think she was fragile, she kept her complaints to herself, doing her best to focus on the rolling hills of Nanir and the different people they passed on the winding road.

Nanir was green and captivating with the late summer. Near Mithe the hills were sharp and angular, but as they traveled east they developed into gentle curves with shallow valleys. The farms were broader and dotted with planted trees. Occasionally, the valleys had trees clumped together, though most of the hills were bare and open.

Merchants of many shades and shapes passed by. Orla, having become used to the variety of people living in Mithe had learned not to stare, There were religious men making pilgrimages to different temples in the hills, and local villagers joining one another for harvest festivals. Shifty men would pass and Darragh or Ternell would ride closer to Orla while casting them watchful glances. Orla thought this was excessive given that every passing group took more notice of Chusa than the rest of them.

Chusa was his own parade. He preferred to run instead of ride, which was fortunate since the stable master had nothing large enough to carry a drasta. Darragh had offered to split the cost to rent a single man cart with two horses, but Chusa refused.

He jogged along side them and never seemed to tire. If they passed a merchant or pilgrim along the road whom he knew he would stop to chat and sprint to catch up later in the day. He called out to people passing in different languages and sung songs to pass the long mid-day hours. People seemed to know him all along the way and the attention he drew made Darragh uncomfortable.

Late in the afternoon on the first day, Orla heard a group of slender humanoids loudly whisper comments about Chusa as they passed. It reminded Orla of the exchange at the inn and she slowed to speak with Ternell; careful to keep outside Chusa's hearing.

"May I ask you something?"

"Of course, lass. What else are we going to do?"

"What did Darragh mean when he told Chusa he had a chance," Orla paused to think. "How did he put it...? To prove them wrong? To gain some trust?"

"Ah well. That's not an easy question to answer." Ternell shifted in his saddle while he thought, as if it would help him to order his ideas. Throughout the conversation every time he would stop to think he would bring his upper lip into his mouth and comb through the hairs of his mustache with his lower teeth. Orla had never noticed this habit before and did what she could to not be distracted by it.

"Drasta, as a species, like coasts and water, much like their dragon cousins. The city of Naynor is very old, much older than the monks and sages who work to record history, so no one knows how old for sure. Depending on whose story you believe, one or the other was there first.

Ternell paused and raked his mustache with his teeth. "Being that the drasta are much older, I think it's probably them." He made another brief pause, "But who am I to say."

"What others? Who other than the drasta?"

"I'm gettin' to that part...it's not an easy thing to explain and you have to guess at what you think really happened." He paused again to rake his mustache. "My best guess is, back when the drasta were an unsettled tribe and they traveled loosely together, they used to go up and down the coast. One year, upon returning to their summer homes, they found that a group had settled there to form a new village." Darragh chuckled with a thought and turned to Orla.

"I'm sure from Chusa's temper you can imagine how they reacted." Into his mouth went his upper lip. "Each side claims they tried to find a peaceful solution, but even if they did the village grew over time. The drasta were pushed further and further south.

"Now. Ugh, this part I don't know too much about." Ternell seemed a bit uncomfortable. "But, ugh, as I understand it... drasta mate in the summer. So you can see how it would be an important time to be settled. It was very disruptive... They couldn't mate... Over the years their numbers dwindled down and they blamed the elves and humans in Naynor. They started to hate them and tried to drive them away.

"They set fires and destroyed roads. Naynor has been big on trade for some time and most of our merchants still come through there. Since then, they just kept fighting and they still do. The drasta have a settlement on the coast not far from Naynor, but they feel that they have a right to the city. The humans and elves from Naynor say that they deserve to be there

90

too and because of the attacks that occasionally happen drasta are banned from the city after dark... It's not an easy situation for either side.

"For a long time many in-land people hated drasta too, for no reason... but Chusa has been a big part of changing that. He and his people decided that he would move from home and travel, let people see that the drasta aren't all bad..."

Orla nodded and Ternell paused. No wonder the council from Naynor thought some drasta were behind the fires. Orla looked over to Chusa; he was trying to get a group of monks to sing with him about traveling along the road; they seemed frightened but were going along with it. Though he could be loud and obnoxious she couldn't see him hurting innocent people who had done nothing to him personally.

"Ah, but don't worry." Orla was pulled from her mental wandering. "We'll find other evidence and we'll prove it's not them. Don't fret, lass."

Orla had to smile at Ternell, he seemed to always see how things could turn out well. He talked often of his path in life and was so sure if it. Orla was a bit jealous of his clear footing.

By nightfall the first day Orla's entire body hurt, and after sleeping on the hard ground it was worse. She woke stiffly, roused by the sun and the smell of breakfast being cooked in the large travelers encampment off the road. They ate, packed, and set out again to the east, keeping an eye for trees in the distance.

On their second day of steady travel, just before mid-day, the cleared fields gave way to young trees. The road was wide here and as they ambled on the trees were thicker and healthy. Ahead the road continued into the darkness under the canopy for some time.

Orla had never seen a forest so large. In the distance it followed the road until a hill crested and she couldn't see any further. On the plateau trees were short and in small clumps, you could pass through them in a few minutes. They had little wood and built most homes out of sod or brick. Yet again, Orla had to remind herself not to gawk and closed her mouth as she looked around.

It wasn't long before they saw scorch marks and areas where the trees burnt out. Darragh cautioned Orla and Lorcian to watch for anything unusual and that they had the rest of the day to ride.

Since the last town before the forest the road was empty. Their group had become quiet, even Chusa, and they could hear animals moving in the forest. Orla felt uncomfortable in such a closed natural setting, there was so little sky and it she felt like something was watching her every movement and breath. She couldn't resist the urge to look over her shoulders every few moments and glance around.

Orla didn't want the others in the party to see how uncomfortable she was and fell behind. *You're just being silly.*

There's nothing out there. While chastising herself Orla glanced down.

Just off the road a pile of brush had been pulled together at the base of a few trees. At a quick glance it looked like a rise at the edge of the path. She wouldn't have noticed it at all, except there was a large, thick arrow carved in the ground pointing at the pile. It was half a gold-piece deep and wide; very deliberate and unbroken, as if someone had just dug it out. Orla stopped and squinted, unsure if this was worth noting. She decided caution was safer, even if it ended in embarrassment.

"Darragh. Come look at this." No sooner had Orla spoken then Chusa let out a loud, deep-throated growl.

Orla turned sharply and her horse began to dance with her unease. Chusa had been struck with a large pot of a thick, oily substance. It dripped from his shoulders and oozed over his arms, weighing him down and multiplying itself, spreading further down his body.

For a moment they were all caught off guard watching Chusa struggle. Darragh stepped toward him and then a group of gray-skinned, foul smelling creatures leapt from the trees. Most were the size of a small human man, though one was much larger. They each wore thin, scuffed leather armor and carried a few simple weapons. As soon as they appeared they yelled and charged forward.

The largest one came from the trees too near to Darragh's horse, startling it. It kicked back a few times, catching the creature in the chest and throwing Darragh to the ground. Both

93

Darragh and the monster struggled to their feet and came at the other, though it was obvious that Darragh was more handicapped by the fall than the creature by the kick.

Three of the creatures surrounded Lorcian and Ternell. They circled the horses and reached at them with spears. Lorcian and Ternell did their best to deflect the attacks with short swords.

Not far from them another, even smaller, creature poked the nearly incapacitated Chusa with a short spear. To Chusa it most likely felt like a human being poked with a tooth pick: more of an annoyance then painful.

Orla was transfixed, her horse dancing under her. She had felt unprepared before they left Mithe and here she was, proving herself right. *What can I do? If Darragh can't beat them...*

"Orla, do something!" Darragh struggled to call while grappling with the grotesque creature. The monster had Darragh by the shoulder and was overpowering him, "Orla!" He called louder.

Orla nodded absentmindedly and struggled to concentrate. Breathing carefully she raised her hands, closed her eyes, and flicked her fingertips all at once. She opened her eyes to see what had happened.

All the monsters were now soaking wet. It seemed that Orla had conjured water and dropped it on them. This didn't help. It didn't seem to deter them in any way as if they barely noticed it had happened.

"ORLA!" Darragh ordered. "Do something USEFUL!"

Orla shut her eyes and breathed deeper and slower. Heaving her chest and trying not to lose control. Darragh's yelling snapped through her thoughts again.

"NOW! Do something NOW!"

"OK!" Orla yelled back and flipped her whole wrists out.

The struggling stopped. Orla slowly opened her eyes and saw that the creatures had all stopped moving. Her friends stood staring at the enemies that moments before had threatened them. Darragh laughed uncomfortably and tried to remove himself from the grip of the monster. He broke a few of its fingers with a loud *crunch* and stepped back.

"Well done, Orla." He limped a few steps closer as Orla dismounted. "I knew you would think of something."

Orla also chuckled in a strange falsetto. Lorcian and Ternell were also dismounting and poking at nearby creatures. Ternell let out a puff of air.

"Lass. They're frozen solid." He turned to Orla in awe. He moved a few paces closer to Orla and Lorcian followed.

"That's cold of you." Lorcian said with a crooked smile. "Cold." He repeated. Orla wasn't sure if it was a compliment or a curse. Orla's eyes were still wide with shock and she worried what her friends were thinking.

"What were they?" She exclaimed and Ternell stepped closer.

"Goblins, lass. Though no telling what they were up so far out."

"I've seen them in the woods before," Darragh interjected, "but they normally don't attack unless they want something or know you have something good to steal. It's obvious that we don't."

As Orla tried to wrap her brain around this new information a low, throaty growl caught everyone's attention.

"Chusa!" From the neck down Chusa was covered in a sticky goo that completely prohibited movement. Orla quickly went to work blasting him with water to soak away the substance. "I'm so sorry we forgot you!"

"Well, I wouldn't want to interrupt the lesson." While Orla worked Chusa relaxed and smiled. "Didn't you say you've only just been at Eolas? This is impressive for a new student." Orla blushed. She'd never been complimented by a half-dragon before.

When Chusa was free he stepped close to the goblin who had been harassing him with the spear.

"Disgusting things." He muttered, putting his hand up to dismiss it. Chusa mis-gauged the placement of his hand and smacked the goblin. The frozen body fell over with a loud SMASH! Millions of small pieces of the frozen goblin exploded and spread across the packed-earth road. Orla let out a low scream and stepped back.

"Little wizard," he marveled, "You didn't just freeze them outside. You froze all the water all the way through them."

The others had been searching the area for clues and stopped at the sound of the body shattering. Now they came in closer to Chusa and Orla. Darragh took it all in.

"Chusa, you help the other two search the goblin bodies. Be mindful and move them into the forest when you're done." He leaned closer to Orla.

"And you. When you use your gift so close to us like that, keep your eyes open. Less of a chance of someone getting hurt that way." Darragh smiled then. It was strange to Orla that he would be so at home in Mithe, as so differently at peace in the strange forest.

Lorcian brought a satchel back to them.

"Not much worth anything; but I found these, and they weren't on the other ones." Lorcian opened his hand to show three thin, small vials that appeared to be empty. Chusa had come up behind them while Lorcian spoke.

"Well, lets just open 'em up." He reached through Darragh and Orla but she stepped in.

"No! We don't know what's in them. Maeve always says to examine first and open something like this when you're sure what's going on."

"But they're just vials." He argued back.

"They're magical." She picked them up in her hand and looked closer. "I can't tell what, but I can feel it. And look at the cork." A seal was burnt into the cork with two concentric circles surrounding a jagged line. "They were sealed with a burn. Just

97

wait and I'll figure it out."

Chusa made a noise that sounded like a scoff in his throat and turned away. Darragh smiled down at Orla in a reassuring way and then urged them all back onto their horses, the goblin bodies now disposed of.

Chapter Nine

With the demonstration of her own power Olra relaxed and began to look about, not for enemies, but at the forest itself. She was alert but less afraid knowing she could defend herself with more than poor dagger work.

The forest was increasingly beautiful as they moved deeper during the afternoon. Wind passed through the outstretched branches over the road and leaves tumbled loose. Birds swung through the air around them and a foal deer paused in a clearing to graze. It seemed to Orla that just as quickly as the afternoon began, it was passing.

Darragh stopped abruptly and turned from the road, leading them on what seemed to be a foot path. Orla was convinced it wasn't wide enough to hold them and the horses, but trusted Darragh enough to follow. She was wrong, it was an optical illusion and after a few feet the path turned sharply and could accommodate them all. They moved into a gully that wasn't visible from the road and as they descended the village unfolded below. The village of Ni'Ca seemed to appear out of the forest itself.

Children peaked out from behind trees along the path and giggled. They played with large hoops and sticks seeing who could roll the furthest, and some came to laugh, taunt, and talk with them. The adults in the village seemed indifferent, though as they approached the clearing in the center of the village a group of Irwu came to join them.

The Irwu were paler than Orla expected. From Ternell's description of the way they lived, most of their time was spent outside. She had expected them to be tan but it seemed a life in the forest kept them mostly out of the sun. Most were barefoot and some bare chested, though it didn't seem to matter to them if it was a man or woman. As they dismounted a young man stepped forward.

He was average height and lanky with long, thin limbs. He wore a simple vest of woven flax and pants of deer hide. He had jewelry made of drilled nuts and bone and rings of carved and polished stone.

"Welcome," he said in a light accent with round, long vowels. He reached forward to Chusa and gave a simple greeting. The man gripped Chusa's arm just inside his elbow and touched the outside of the elbow with his other hand. Chusa rested his fingertips on the outside of the mans elbow as well. He moved to Lorcian and then Ternell and greeted each of them the same. Next was Darragh and the young man paused to look him in the eye.

"Hello, old friend," this man had a strange look in his eye and a light smile. He cut the distance and they pulled one another into a familiar hug. When they broke from the hug the man turned to Orla.

"Welcome to the Irwu wood. I am called Jak and this village is Ni'Ca." He reached out his arm and Orla shook it as the men had done. "Is this your first time in the Irwu?"

"Yes. It's very beautiful."

"I agree." Jak stepped aside and introduced the others in his party: Nan'ath, Eath, and Pa'l. Each shook as Jak had done and welcomed them. Jak explained that Nan'ath was the highest ranking woman in the village and the most honored decision maker. Eath was her daughter and served as both adviser and assistant and Pa'l an accomplished warrior. Jak explained later that this was an honorary title as they'd not been to war in some time.

He gave them a tour of the village as the sun began to set. Fires were being stoked for light and cast shadows up into the canopy. Chusa, Ternell, and Lorcian joined, eager to walk out the tension in their bodies from riding. Darragh had started out following them and Orla didn't notice when he fell behind.

As they followed Jak he stopped to chat with different villagers in their native language. It was thick and heavy with vowels and Orla couldn't follow what they were saying; from their gestures she guessed it was friendly gossip.

The village was larger than Orla had originally thought and marveled at how small it seemed, even from inside. The Irwu

101

tribesmen had used the forest in harmony with their structures. Hut frames were built by stripping young trees, poling them into the ground, and gradually bending them in together with a large band. Once they were able to be tied together, stripped branches were used to create a lattice and then bark was laid over the top. Each element was tied with a bit of hide or stripped sapling lanyard.

Many structures were built around trees and Jak's hut used two that grew close together. They formed a natural door and split his hut into two rooms. One had an old fox hole beneath it that he'd expanded into a literal root cellar.

Most of the huts were on the forest floor; however a defense system was constructed above in the trees. Jak turned to Orla.

"Did you wonder where Darragh was going when he turned onto the little path?" She was caught off guard and embarrassed to be singled out.

"Yes. I thought we'd notice a village this size. I didn't realize it was set off the road."

"That's what your supposed to think." He smiled and began to move on down the path. "Did you know that this is the only Irwu village with a name?"

"No."

"It's also the only village known to outsiders. Every other village is hidden; we like to trade with your people, but we like to protect our way, too."

Orla smiled at their ingenuity. They'd learned to shield

themselves from the outside world without the benefit of magic.

"The forest helps, though we have been having a hard time understanding about the fires. The forest is confused and it's scaring my people."

They reached the end of a lane of huts and Jak gestured wide with his arm. Orla looked up to see rows of tents and a few new huts being constructed.

"Refugees. The fires have destroyed many of the outer villages. All of the remaining villages have taken in as many as they can. We try to believe that the forest will provide for us."

"Tell us about the forest and the fires." After listening for most of the tour Ternell piped up.

"Why don't we gather everyone for a meal and I can share what we've been able to figure out."

Jak lead the group back to his hut and there Nan'ath was seated at a low table. Darragh was already waiting for them while Eath, Pa'l, and two others were setting out a meal. There were mats on the floor; Jak sat next to Darragh and the others filled out the spaces around the table.

Dinner consisted of five simple courses. A broth soup spiced with zested citrus fruit and a leek native to this region of the forest. A salad consisting mostly of a bitter root and a hot pepper that each of them tried and none could eat but Jak and Nan'ath. Jak explained that it improved vitality and gave two more to each of them to nibble on. Next were steaks of wild boar that had been roasting the entire day. Then a seed pod as large as a fist that was cracked open and full of a rich, sweet milk and finally, an orange berry crushed and served over a thick cake for desert.

Though she wasn't able to clean her plate, Orla tried everything. She ate most of the soup and all of the berry cake. It was all served with a thick beer that Orla slipped but didn't care for; Ternell, however, drank glass after glass.

"This could pass for dwarven beer in some circles," he marveled and seemed genuinely impressed; he and one of Nan'eth's assistants got into a deep conversation about a local plant that was similar to the hops used in dwarven ale. Orla heard his breathy, "Fascinating," from time to time, but wasn't really listening.

As the food began to settle and conversation lulled, Jak brought their focus to why they had come.

"My people," he began carefully with a look to Nan'eth, "believe we have upset a spirit of the forest and it is taking revenge. There are many arguments as to what we may have done, yet I believe there is another answer.

"The forest has done little to explain what is happening. There are many kinds creatures kinds in this forest, some magical and others not. It's possible that any of them could be involved; though I have a hard time believing that an inhabitant of the Irwu wood would hurt it. I can share with you what we know as facts and will do my best not to color it with local lore." Jak settled in and straightened his shoulders while he gathered his thoughts.

"As I said, there are many kinds here and at places along the trading road there are camps. Some are for travelers and some of the deeper camps are for thieves and brigands. Most of the fires have begun at these camps, though some are set away from them. They don't seem to follow a pattern and most seem to be near humans."

Orla wondered what else was in the forest that they could be near, and and what he meant when he said the forest talked with him.

"The forest is a very confused place right now. It talks about little men that it has not mention before and the areas near the fire are so devastated that I can't get any information.

"The most recent fire was set just a few days ago. It was very close to a thieves' encampment and I believe it to have been a target, but there's also a village nearby. Fortunately, the fire burnt out before it could spread that far.

"I'd like to take you there tomorrow. You'll be the only non-Irwu to ever see it." He looked to Darragh. "Our elders have agreed that we can trust you."

The evening didn't last much longer. With dinner finished and the weight of the long day of travel settling in, they became quiet. Eath and Pa'l rose and requested Orla, Chusa, Ternell, and Lorcian to follow them. Orla looked back at Darragh, confused that he would not be coming with them.

"It's alright, Orla." He said in a low, calm voice. "These

people are friends."

Orla turned to go and Nan'eth joined her. As Orla held the curtain in the entry way back for the old wise woman, she glimpsed Darragh and Jak with their heads low together engaged in serious conversation. She let the curtain fall, and through the fog of tiredness, followed the others to a hammock in a hut set aside for their visit.

Chapter Ten

Orla woke much earlier than normal and felt the stab of pain in her neck when she looked to her left. The hammock didn't agree with her, having slept almost every night of her life on beds of straw or feathers.

Trying to get out, she stumbled and kicked Ternell, finding him on the floor. He muttered in his sleep and rolled over, unphased by the knock to his ribs. *How did I get up there last night?* She thought as she headed toward the door.

There was little movement in the village as few were awake. The late summer sun dawned slowly through the trees and in this moment between the night and coming day, Orla wondered if the forest would speak to her, too. As she stood next to the door of their hut Darragh emerged from Jak's with his pants' front loose and without a shirt.

Orla felt the familiar glow in her cheeks and tried not to think about her mentor without his shirt. She stood still and watched him walk to the latrine. He disappeared for a few moments and, after reemerging, made his way back toward the hut. At the door he met Jak and the two embraced. Orla smiled at understanding a little more about their leader. She turned back in the hut and hunted for the bedroll in her pack. Unfurling it, she joined Ternell on the ground.

A few hours later, when everyone was dressed and packed, they set out. The paths in the woods were too narrow for horses and as Jak preferred a slow progress to allow him to commune with the forest, they walked.

Through the hours of the morning they wound their way in and out of underbrush on the narrow paths. They spoke very little and even Chusa let the quiet peace of the forest calm him. The forest deepened and the canopy obstructed more and more of the mid-day light. Through the undergrowth of the old forest they could see light breaking up ahead.

"We'll be stopping in this village for rest," Jak called over his shoulder. "As I mentioned last night, many of my people have never met outsiders. I've done what I can to prepare them. Don't be surprised if they are odd around you."

Jak led them to the clearing at the outskirts of town and a

few children that were playing near the forest edge ran toward the huts, yelling in the Irwu language.

From the cluster of huts appeared a mix of adult Irwu and some of them came forward to greet Jak. Others stayed just inside their doors and watched while a few of the children bravely strode forward to investigate the strangers.

The children were especially intrigued with Ternell and Chusa. Having never seen non-Irwu it was doubtful they knew about dwarves and drasta. Ternell chuckled and reached his hand out toward them. They might have approached, were it not for Chusa. He stood just over Ternell's shoulder and watched the children awkwardly. They had stopped short of Ternell, looking from the dwarf's bearded grin to the drasta's confused expression. It appeared that Chusa had little experience with children; he attempted a smile and, despite himself, the children scattered.

The Irwu leaders exchanged the arm-shake Orla learned the previous evening with Jak, then each of them shook at the elbow with the outsiders. Due to the language barrier, no one spoke.

The eldest of the group turned to Jak , who listened and translated.

"They have prepared a meal for us and would like to bless us before we continue," Jak paused and let out a gentle sigh. "They believe it will help us overcome the angry spirits."

Orla and the others nodded, trying to help Jak feel more comfortable. If it didn't bother them, maybe it would bother him less. Orla was also curious to know that an Irwu blessing would be like, though she tried to mask her excitement.

They were escorted into the village where they met an older woman and a few younger companions. The older woman, San, was this village's elder. She was younger and shorter than Nan'eth, the elder in Ni'Ca, and through Jak's translation she greeted them. Orla read the concern in her face while San expressed how grateful she was for their visit.

The fire had obviously unnerved them and at its mention Orla realized she could smell ash and smoke in the air. She didn't remember the first time she smelt it, though as she thought back over the last two days it seemed to have followed them throughout the forest. The beautiful woods reeked of burnt-out fires.

San moved toward one of the larger huts and gestured for them to follow. The hut functioned both as her home and a meeting place. Inside a simple meal of dried meat and foraged foods was set for them. While eating Orla scanned the room.

Many practical goods were piled along the walls. Bowls, pipes, tools, and other stored items. She was surprised to see some armor and weapons, obviously from the outside human world, stored on a set of shelves in a far corner. She asked Jak about them.

"While the villages of the forest rarely see visitors that, doesn't mean they do not appreciate the benefits of trade."

"But why weapons?"

"Our outer villages train young warriors and hunters should the need for them ever arise. While we are not an aggressive people, we are very good at defending ourselves; and the forest helps. When the warriors are ready they are sent to Ni'Ca to learn

110

about the outside world."

Orla was about to ask how the forest helped when she was interrupted by the appearance of two Irwu. One was very old and the other looked to be in her twentieth year. They looked very similar and Orla assumed they were father and daughter.

Both had long, straight hair to their waists and hazel eyes like Jak. Their noses were flatter than the people in Mithe and they were more slight. They wore jewelry from the forest and some of metal, and each had grasses woven into their long hair and hollowed nuts on strings tied to their ankles. The shells hit one another as they walked, making a hollow 'thunk' when they moved.

Orla recognized the focused expressions of the Irwu version of a wadima; these were a medicine man and woman, come to bless the party.

They said nothing as they entered and faced one another. Each carried a mask carved from bark in their hands. The older man nodded and turned around and the young woman lifted the mask and fastened it to his head. Their breathing was even and deep as if they were meditating in motion.

After the woman finished tying on the mask, the man turned back to face her, took her mask, and she turned while he fastened it for her. She turned back and they stood, masked and facing one another, for a few moments. A breeze swept through the walls of the hut and the air changed. The two turned suddenly toward the group.

The two chanted and danced. They jerked their bodies in

111

rhythm to their stomping feet while moving toward the group. They swept wide arms over each of the travelers and touched their shoulders lightly. To Orla's surprise, Jak became very tense when it was his turn, though he said nothing.

When they reached Orla first the old man, then the woman tapped her on the shoulder. Their fingers brushed lightly on top where the bones came together. Though it may have been her imagination, Orla felt warmer and stronger at the connection. She was rejuvenated and her mind felt clear with thought and purpose.

They completed the shoulder taps and moved back to where they had started by the door. They stood facing one another and allowed their breathing to return to the meditative pattern it had before. Then the woman reached for the mask of the man and removed it. He removed her's as well and they left.

Through Jak's translation, San thanked them for coming. She rose and led them to the far side of the village where the path continued. Everyone other than Jak and Darragh seemed jarred by the abrupt change from the blessing to leaving, but followed until they were just out of earshot. Orla moved to catch up with Jak.

"Was that the blessing?"

"Yes."

"What were they saying?"

For the first time since Orla met him, Jak seemed annoyed to have been bothered with her questions.

"First they cleansed the air. Then they asked the spirits of the forest to watch over each of us. That's why they touched us. They were giving some power to each of us."

Orla paused to consider this and Jak's aggravated tone.

"Do you know them?"

"Yes. They are my father and sister."

"Oh." Orla looked back toward the village and wondered why he didn't speak with them before he had left. She realized that it was Jak's village they just passed through. *Why didn't he stop? Why didn't he talk to them?* She thought it better not to ask and fell behind him as they continued to trek.

As they walked the smells of ash and smoke thickened and after a short time they reached a clearing. Jak, Darragh, and Chusa slowed and fanned out to allow the others to enter beside them.

They stood on the edge of a burnt out clearing and scorched plants crunched beneath their feet. The smell of freshly charred wood hung in the air and the trees to either side of the clearing were singed. Darragh turned to the rest:

"We'll search the area and learn anything we can," He looked down at the burnt grasses and mumbled to himself, "if there's anything left."

The clearing crested a shallow hill, not quite high enough to see over the tops of nearby trees. Orla followed the tree line around the crest of the hill and below to where the ground leveled out. She reached the bottom of the hill and her breath caught in her throat. A few paces in front of her was a small boulder. It had a crack in the front and one edge was flat with a ledge that was all too familiar.

She glanced about the clearing. Her companions were making a more thorough search than she, sweeping the open spaces in a grid pattern to be sure nothing was missed. The closest was Chusa and she called him over.

"Can you lift me up there?" She gestured to the ledge.

He came closer and looked toward the boulder. "I can look up there for you," and he started to reach.

"No, no." She boldly stepped in front of him, much closer to him than she'd been before. "Please. I'll go."

She wasn't really sure why it had to be her or what she could expect to find. *What will I tell them if there's anything up there?*

Chusa carefully wrapped his scaly, clawed hands around her waist and lifted her to the ledge with ease. She gripped the edge and pulled her chin over. As her face cleared the lip she was met with the charred goblin body, the blacked eyes peering into her own. Without a moment to steady herself, Orla screamed. Chusa dropped her into his arms and she buried her face in his shoulder.

"Shh, little wizard. What is it?"

114

Darragh, Lorcian, and Ternell, summoned by the sound of her scream, ran over the hill. Lorcian was last to clear the hill and once he saw that there was no immediate danger he slowed, disappointed.

"What happened?" Darragh demanded.

"Nothing." Orla dismissed him as Chusa set her on her feet. She didn't want to admit she was shaken up by the body. She looked up to the drasta and ordered him, "Chusa, lift me up again."

"But one of us can go."

"Just lift!" she demanded, surprised by her own braveness.

Chusa sighed, which sounded like a growl, and lifted Orla again. She grabbed the edge and pulled herself all the way up.

The goblin didn't seem charred enough to have died from the fire, though his hands were streaked with ash and feet charred. His face was frozen in a terrified expression and some scavenging birds had torn through his clothing and desecrated other parts of him.

Orla took a deep, open mouthed gasp, held her breath, and knelt beside him.

"What is it?" Darragh yelled up.

"A goblin," she choked, "It looks like he was caught in the fire and stuck up here."

"How'd you know where to look?"

"Lucky guess." Orla had no intention of telling them about her dream and would do her best to avoid it.

115

He had simple armor and short spear similar to the goblins from the ambush. A hide satchel with crude stitching was still slung across his body. Orla wanted to spend as little time on the ledge as possible, so bringing the pouch down with her would be ideal.

I'm not touching that thing. She told herself: *I have limits.* She looked around the ledge, paused to think, and remembered: since the night she had the goblin vision she couldn't shake the fear that if magic ever failed she would be helpless. She'd been keeping a dagger in her boot, just in case.

She went to work with the knife and after a few moments the strap was cut and the bag was free. A quick check of the rest of the ledge revealed nothing else of value. Orla peered over the edge to Chusa.

"Leap down and I'll catch you." He was trying to be supportive, but even though Chusa's smile was not intentionally threatening, it was like an alligator asking you over for dinner.

Orla glanced down at the cut satchel and quickly tied the two halves of the strap back together. *Wearing a dead goblin's bag might be as bad as touching the body,* she thought as she brought the strap over her head. She hung from the ledge and dropped into his up-stretched hands.

As he lowered her to the ground Lorcian joined them. While Orla had been on the ledge he had became bored and had wandered off.

"I found something," Lorcian held out a few broken pieces of glass. Darragh took them from him, looked them over, and moved the three largest pieces close enough to see it was a vial.

"Orla, may I have the vials from yesterday." It wasn't a question. She produced them and placed them in his outstretched hand. Side by side it was clear that the vials were the same size and shape.

He stood and thought for some time; tracing leads in his mind and arriving at no conclusions. He turned them over and tried from different angles, waiting for inspiration to strike. Eventually the others became bored; Lorcian wandered off again and Chusa sat, but Orla, Jak, and Ternell loyally stood, waiting. Finally, Orla broke the near-silence of the clearing.

"May I see them?" Darragh glanced at her, always hard to read, and placed the bits of glass into her hand.

Orla sighed to herself; she'd been dreading this moment. She knew she would have to tell them about her visions eventually and wanted desperately for it to go well. She had considered telling Darragh separately before the others found out, but it seemed now they would all learn together.

She decided it was best to do it when it helped them. She reached to the chain around her neck and pulled the amethyst from below her shirt. Darragh narrowed his eyes at it and looked up to her face but she did not meet his eyes. Hers were downcast and focused on the ground.

She slipped the chain over her had and reached her hand to Ternell.

"Would you hold this?" She didn't lift her eyes, already knowing the answer. Her other hand was around the vial and the moment the chain left her fingertips the vision flashed to her.

It had been months since her last waking vision and Orla was immediately struck by two things: the clarity of it, and the new-found control.

First she was hit with a wave of sight, the familiar fear brought on by the older woman dancing in fire; but she was able to push it away with her mind.

She focused instead on the connection to the glass in her hand. It was as if an invisible cord of energy was running from the vials, into her hand, and up to her mind. The energy was made up of the power in the vial and the absence of it in the broken glass. Focusing on the broken glass, she could see the clearing, though in the vision it was still healthy and the greens of the grass were silver in a bath of moonlight.

Near the crest of the hill, not far from where she stood, there were goblins. They piled dead branches and dried leaves. Some had carried kindling and hay from their camp. She counted a total of six.

Directing the workers was a goblin she felt a strong connection to. She squinted to see him more sharply and in a flash she was seeing through his eyes. Orla recognized the familiarity of having been him in her dream; his height, the weight of his feet, and feeling of his armor against his leathery skin. The glass in her hand was now the vial in his and she was instructing the other goblins to finish the pile and then stand back.

Outside her mind Orla could hear Lorcian return and ask what she was doing. Ternell silenced him dismissively, but Orla paid them little attention. She couldn't allow herself the distraction and didn't want to consider yet what they would think of the new skills she was demonstrating.

The goblins under her command gathered behind her and, with the tip of her spear, she carved a long arrow in the ground. It pointed at the pile and the tail, straight and long, reached toward the rock. After a brief look to the sky and a gauge of distance she smashed the vial at the end of the arrow tail.

A great crash of lightning hit half way between the vial and the pile of brush. A rush of energy surged down the arrow and lit the pile in a blue, magical fire. A few of the goblins jumped and yelled in surprise. She could feel her goblin self laughing at their fear. "Weaklings," she thought.

They turned to leave. The fire had caught and was spreading, aided by the spell in the vial. She stood to watch for a few moments to ensure that the blaze was spreading.

One of the other goblins looped back into the clearing. He came behind her, and though Orla knew he was there the leader did not see him. With a blow to the back of his head the leader fell to the ground while Orla stayed standing, now observed him from above.

The attacker left, and Orla watched the fire catch on near-by trees. She stood in the fire, reaching out her fingers to the flames without being burnt.

The goblin leader woke on the ground and found himself surrounded by fire. It was singeing his face and the smoke coked him. Knowing what was coming, Orla loosened her grip on the vials and let the vision slip away while she gasped for a deep breath of fresh air.

"They're for calling lightning." She burst out, grasping at

119

Ternell for her amulet. She was tired and working hard to focus on keep the unwelcome fire sorceress at bay. With the amethyst in hand relief washed over her again and she opened her eyes to focus.

"The goblins," she managed, "they're summoning lightening to set fires." She breathed deeply, clearing the feeling of smoke and ash from her chest.

"I'll show you." She walked closer to the base of the hill. "Here." Orla pointed at a gouge in the ground, and now that Orla pointed it out, the arrow was obvious. Tracing it with here eyes, she found burnt bits of the cork from the vial and looked up to Lorcian.

"Is this where you found the glass?"

Lorcian stood with Ternell, Jak, and Chusa, all dumbstruck. Darragh was behind them with his typical smile, he was the only one who recognized what had happened and had a leader's appreciation for it. He stepped between Ternell and Lorcian to meet Orla.

"Perhaps we should explain it to them first?" he suggested.

Orla didn't know the words for it or how they would react. She didn't want to be bothered with telling their futures and she was already exhausted. "It's an unusual gift, Orla. You'll want to explain it."

"Umm." She stumbled to find the words for what she'd just seen. "I can... see things... sometimes. That's how I knew about the goblin body. Well, not that I saw it just now. I saw it awhile ago...in a dream. But the vials, they showed me what happened...he was their leader..."

She pointed to the boulder and with the mention of the corpse she remembered the satchel across her chest.

"Oh!" She exclaimed, wanting to change the subject. She pulled the satchel over her head. "I found this up there."

Orla quickly opened the satchel. Inside were a few more vials and some coins, which she handed to Darragh. In a pocket in the lining was a folded piece of parchment. Orla opened it carefully and held it out for everyone to see.

It was a map of the forest, pocked with circles. They dotted the forest in no particular pattern and some circles were crossed through.

"The Xs are where the fires have been set." Jak reached forward and pointed to a spot deep into the northeast quarter of the forest. "This one without the X is where we are now."

Orla studied the map with the others. There were two sections without marks, one at the south and one far to the north.

"Jak, what's here?" Orla pointed to southern area.

"Very little. It's mostly swamp there, and very few camps. It's hard to travel through, so even the thieves avoid it."

"And here?" She pointed to the north.

"Hills. It's a much older part of the forest so the trees are thicker and larger."

"No Irwu villages? Nothing specific?"

"No. It's too far away from our other settlements so we don't travel there often; only for some rituals and specific celebrations."

Orla thought for a moment and looked up at Darragh, standing over her shoulder. "We should go here." She said decisively.

"Another vision?"

"No. Just logical. Why would you light a fire near your own camp?"

Darragh gave her another of his unreadable smiles.

"Clever." He turned to Jak, "How long will we need to travel there?"

"It's another day in." He hesitated and glanced at Orla. "We may want to stay the night in the village. Our talented friend looks weary."

Orla realized that she was indeed very tired. Even the thought of walking back to the village seemed overwhelming.

"Yes. I think that's best." Darragh said with absolute authority. Chusa gave Orla another of his frightening smiles.

"I'll could carry you back, Little Wizard." Orla suddenly felt a bit better.

"Oh. Umm. No, thank you."

Orla returned to the village in a haze of near exhaustion. When she thought of how much further she had to walk, even the next few steps seemed to overwhelm her; so she chose to think of nothing.

Later she couldn't remember the walk or arriving at the village. She had no memory of returning to San's hut or falling asleep with the afternoon sun filtering though leaves and playing across her blankets. She shivered with fever despite the summer heat.

She did remember waking in the early evening. The sun was setting and even the gentle light hurt her eyes, jabbing at her brain. She lifted her head and heard what sounded like "Eeee k'nee." A hand tried to gently push her back to her mat while another pushed a bowl into her hands. The voice said more clearly

"A'iee ha'nee. Na haau." Orla focused on the young woman above her and the hand gestures she made clearly with each word. With 'aiu' she pointed to Orla, 'hanee' to the bowl and gestured drinking, for 'na haau' she pointed with her two smaller fingers to the center of Orla's forehead, just above her eyes.

"She felt your headache and made you some medicine."

Orla raised her head to see Darragh in the doorway.

"You speak their language?" Orla's voice sounded distant through the sensory fog of the headache.

"I've been to the main camp many times; I can say simple things. She's telling you to drink it and saying 'headache'."

Orla smelled the bowl and looked inside. It was a greenish-brown thin paste with pieces of a dark leaf and crushed pods that smelled like earth. Orla took a few meager sips and looked up at the woman.

"Don't worry, it's safe. Na'l wouldn't hurt you." Darragh chimed in, smiling and nodding to the woman. Orla huffed at his interference and, sipping, peered over the edge of the shallow bowl to look more closely at the woman. Her eyes focused in the low light and Orla recognized the woman from the blessing earlier in the day. Orla kept her eyes on the woman as she spoke to Darragh.

"Na'l is Jak's sister? The woman from the blessing?"

"Yes." Darragh's face hardened subtly and Orla knew better than to ask more about Jak's family.

"How did she know?"

"About your head?" Orla nodded, "From what Jak has told me about the forest and the Irwu's connection to it, she could feel it. And I bet she knows what it's like to stretch abilities like you did today. You have more in common with her than you think."

The young woman reached for the bowl and, after gently pushing Orla back to her mat, rose to leave.

"How do I say thank you?" Orla asked, already feeling relieved and tired.

"A'iee Gea." Darragh replied gently from the door.

"Aee ghean, Naal." Orla muttered through the fog of near sleep. The young woman turned in the door and smiled as she pulled lose the ties on a curtain at the door. It fell across the entry as Orla drifted into a more peaceful rest.

The morning dawned with a cool fog. Orla rose later than the others, and when she asked why they hadn't woken her and Ternell said gently that she needed the rest.

Jak wasn't with the others waiting outside San's hut. He appeared a few moments later from between two huts, a flush on his usually calm, blank face. He took a breath to steady himself and started to speak, though was quickly interrupted.

Na'l came the same way Jak had, and when he turned to face her they glared at one another for a few tense moments. Orla, Darragh, Ternell and the others looked away.

Eventually the young woman backed down. She looked to each of Jak's companions before stomping back the way she'd come. She didn't seem angry at any of them, though Orla felt as if she had weighed each ones worth and had trouble understanding why. Ternell broke the silence, trying to get past the moment.

"And what was that for?" He blurted to Jak.

"Not everyone agrees that helping you is the right course of action."

"Well, why the Orcus not?"

Jak sighed. It didn't seem that this was something he wanted to discuss, though refusing to answer Ternell would have consequences. Darragh may have led the group, but everyone understood that Ternell was his partner and helped make the important decisions. Darragh trusted him and ignoring him could cause problems.

"The forest is very confused right now," Jak began, "and there are different opinions about what that means." Ternell didn't understand and Jak took the moment to push forward. He stepped closer to Ternell and lowered his voice, "Fortunately, they don't make my judgments for me, or the rest of the Irwu. We'll not be governed by local superstition. Let's go."

Darragh stepped up to Jak.

"This isn't worth your family. I can lead us in the forest."

"There are many kinds of family." Jak held Darragh's gaze.

"Alright." Orla was surprised to see Darragh smile at being challenged like this. "Let's go."

The rest of the morning passed without incident. The weather was warmer and thicker than the last few days and Chusa wilted in the heat. At a stream they stopped to rest and Chusa clumsily dunked his head and shoulders in.

Orla was surprised that Ternell seemed unaffected by the heat, despite his heavy armor and the many layers of padding beneath it. He reached in to the stream to fill his canteen completely at ease. She asked him about it, he glanced back to Chusa, chuckling while his eyes glinted.

"Cooling charm, ma dear." He smiled and reached in his sleeve for a short chain bracelet. A charm dangled from the links, a prism with little white flecks trapped inside, like snowflakes caught in the air. "Got a great deal in Mithe last spring. Quite'a bargain and still one a the best things I ev'r bought. I feel like I'm always hot in tha human lands. Ya all don't have enough hair!"

She smiled and laughed, and in a few moments they were off again. The forest seemed to be more dense as they looked out into it, yet the path was always clear and manageable. It continued to thin as they headed further to the northwest and here there were no roots or other obstacles to trip them, keeping their travel easy.

Orla began to watch Jak more closely and caught him every so often placing his hands on the trees and mumbling. Orla found her way to Darragh's side.

"What's he doing now?" She asked.

"Making sure we get there safely."

Orla watched Jak while they walked and spoke up again.

"Why didn't he do this when we had the horses so we could get here faster? Wouldn't he want us to get there sooner?" Darragh looked down to her and shook his head lightly, as if confounded by such a simple question.

"If your abilities drain you so terribly, what makes you think his will not?"

Orla withered under his gaze and fell back among the others, embarrassed that her reasoning hadn't lived up to Darragh's expectations. In the mid afternoon Jak stopped them with a raise of his hand.

"We're close."

Orla and the others listened but could hear no signs of a nearby camp or the noisy chatter the typically accompanied goblin bands.

"Are you sure..." Lorcian began, but was cut off.

"The trees have lead us here and I trust them. Just wait here."

Jak stepped between two trees and vanished into the underbrush. They gathered where he had disappeared and Orla could see the trail ahead, beyond where he had stopped.

A tangle of roots and brush grew over the path at chest height; at waist height for Chusa. Jak had been working to keep the trail clear by asking the trees for help.

"Yow!" Exclaimed Lorcian at the knot of undergrowth in front of them, "It would take weeks to clear that." He glanced at Orla, "Did you know he could do that?" Orla shook her head in response and after a few moments later Jak returned.

"There is a camp not far ahead with a lot of goblins and a few humans. We're near the back of the camp now and it's pretty tight." Jak looked to Darragh who nodded.

"Show me." Jak lead him ahead and he motioned for the rest to follow.

They crept forward, one by one with Chusa and Ternell in the back. At the edge of the treeline, Jak stopped them and allowed them to approach individually.

A moderately sized camp sprawled before them. Tents enough for twenty goblins stood in clusters around fire pits. A group of three finer tents was set away from the crude goblin structures. Two medium sized tents flanked the entrance to the largest. They could see four humans pacing and talking, three were dressed as warriors and one in clerical robes. Two large, barking dogs were tied to stakes driven between the large tent and each of the medium tents.

There was no fence around the camp, though the back of the larger tents were to a small rock face which gave meager protection. They could attack any open side, though over twenty goblins and any additional resources would be a challenge, even for a group as large as theirs.

Darragh motioned for everyone to follow him and backtracked to the path. Once they were clear of the trees he paced for a few moments and announced: "I have a plan."

"Of course you do," Ternell said; though Darragh chose to ignore the intrusion.

"Orla, are you feeling up to some more magic today?" He looked her in the face with a serious expression.

"Absolutely. That stuff she gave me last night did the trick." Jak raised an eyebrow at this but said nothing.

"Excellent. I want you to go to the other side, near the dark green tent. Keep a safe distance, and light a fire; make an explosion if you can. We need a diversion and the blast should bring the goblins out to the forest. Jak will go with you to keep you safe." Turning to the others, Darragh continued,

"We'll go after the humans; without leaders the goblins will scatter. They'll go back wherever they came from or else Jak's young warriors can drive them out for practice. We only have to get rid of whoever is in those big tents.

"Lorcian, I want you to sneak into the tent. If the priest isn't inside look for any proof you can find and get out. If he is, he doesn't seem like much of a fighter. Kill him.

"Chusa and Ternell, you'll be with me. We'll take the dogs, bodyguards, and any goblins that bother coming back to camp while we're still here; we just keep the tent clear and let the kid do his thing.

"Everybody got it?"

Over the last few days Orla had accomplished so much; proving to herself that she wasn't helpless. She'd killed goblins, hiked the woods, met the Irwu, and found the information they need to get here. They couldn't do all of it without her and she didn't need to be babysat,

"Don't you need Jak's help more than I do? I'm just going to be hiding, I can take care of myself." The others looked at her, surprised to hear her question Darragh so openly; even if gently. Lorcian was the first to reply,

"We'd all feel better if he was with you."

The comment would have annoyed Orla if any of them had said it; but in the unknowingly biting tone of a teenage boy it was far worse. Orla felt like he had told her how inept she was, despite all she'd shown them. She looked around to the others, who were trying not to chuckle.

"Well, fine! If you feel that way." Orla snapped and started into the woods. She stopped halfway in and cocked her head over he shoulder to Darragh. "Just be sure you're ready for my signal." Next she snapped her head to Jak. "Are you coming?"

She didn't wait for an answer and continued, stumbling, into the trees. Jak shrugged to Darragh and followed her.

Chapter Eleven

Not wanting her tantrum to be proof of her incompetence, Orla slowed after a few steps and began to sneak into the underbrush. Jak caught up easily and crept beside her. She had work to do and didn't have time to focus on being angry. They made there was around the outside of the camp and Orla lightly rubbed her thumb and middle finger together, feeling the spot where the fire would start.

Their reaction to her confidence had planted the seed: her anxiety in her abilities was returning, knotting itself below her diaphragm. *Don't doubt it now. You can do this. If you can do it twice by accident, once on purpose shouldn't be hard.*

Orla was so deep in the conversation in her head she didn't notice when Jak raised a hand for her to stop.

"Ooh," she mumbled lowly and bumped into him, lost her

balance, and fell back to the ground. Her shin swung forward and hit him in the ankle, tripping him up. They struggled for a moment to untangle their feet and a pair of goblins broke through the brush.

They yelled in their goblin language, completely undecipherable to Jak and Orla. It sounded like a cross between a sneeze and a dry heave. By their arm motions one might guess they were trying to say "You there. Why are you here?"

Orla screamed and raised her hand mid snap, the goblin to the right burst into flames. The goblin hacked in pain and the other goblin began to run.

"Stop him, Orla!" Jak yelled, and Orla raised her hands and concentrated. There was a moment of hesitation as she gained focus and then the other goblin howled and ignited. His clothes seemed to explode with the force of the flames and the nearby brush caught fire.

"JAK!" she screamed and pointed, running toward the brush.

Orla stomped the flames and swore while Jak pulled his cloak off and dampened the fire. Orla stopped stomping and stepped back, then lowered her head and concentrated. The pressure in the clearing dropped and water materialized above the brush, the body, and Jak. It rained down on them, extinguishing the closest flames, and soaking Jak.

The other body was still burning, but voices were calling from the goblin camp. Despite the language barrier, it was easy to tell they were getting louder and there were many of them. There was little time to run or hide.

Jak stood and dashed for a clump of trees. He kicked his feet out and slid beneath the trees, still visible.

"Orla," he whispered loudly and reached out his hand.

"They can see you!" Orla called back, taking a few steps. "Come on, we need to run."

"Just come HERE." Jak got up on his knees and reached for her, grabbing the cuff of her cloak and pulling her down.

Orla slid down next to him and could still clearly see the two smoldering bodies and the dry grasses near by igniting. If the goblin guards were on their way she would have no time to make another diversion.

Orla propped herself up on her elbows, raised her hands, and focused on the burning body. It exploded, larger than she had intended, and spread the fire to block the path to the goblin camp.

They had another problem: the goblins were close and their cover insufficient.

Jak reached his hands to the two trees closest to the clearing and placed his palms flat on the trunks. He took a deep breath into his chest and mumbled quick and low. The branches of the trees lowered and the plants beneath them grew up and when the foliage reached toward one another it shielding Orla and Jak.

Orla gaped, impressed. She knew he'd been working with the forest to clear the path earlier; but knowing it and seeing it in action were very different.

"Down!" he whispered, grabbing the nape of her neck to push her down. He laid down next to her just as the goblins broke through the trees on the far side of the trail.

The goblins carried sacks made of animal skins full to bursting with water. Jak and Orla watched as they swarmed, dousing the rising flames. Two goblins, both with metal hats and covered in scars, were looking around while the others worked. As the flames were extinguished they found the bodies and began a hacking conversation with one another. Though it sounded to Orla like an argument, it occurred to her that maybe all goblin conversations seemed that way to humans.

The goblin captains gestured to the bodies and to the woods. They called to a group of troops nearby that had just finished dousing some flames and barked orders. The troops fanned out and began to search the trail for tracks.

Orla heard a gentle creak behind her and she and Jak lifted their heads to look. Behind them the trees were lifting their branches to create a route for their escape. Jak smiled and patted the tree next to him in thanks.

"Come on," he whispered.

Near the clearing Darragh, Ternell, Chusa, and Lorcian waited and watched. They crouched at the tree line and scanned for the diversion while they watched scouts and learned what they could about the camp.

A pair of guards took the dogs out to relieve themselves and Ternell glanced to Lorcian. He glanced again, thinking. He shifted from one foot to the other and glanced again.

"You didn't have to talk to her like that, you know."

"Like what?" Lorcian snapped back.

"Like you did. You didn't have to talk to her like we think she's no good. You'd have been in trouble in the woods if it wasn't for her. You should be nicer to her."

"I was-"

"That's enough." Darragh barked quietly. "Just watch for the signal."

"There." Chusa grumbled and pointed. Fire had erupted beyond the tree line, but wasn't where they expected.

"That's not where the signal's supposed to be." Lorcian couldn't help but sound a bit righteous.

"Ya, but it's working anyway." Ternell pointed to the camp. Not far away goblins were scrambling. They were yelling while the humans were barking orders, some in the human language and some that sounded mixed with goblin.

"Why are they here?" Lorcian watched the humans organizing the goblins into a bag brigade to fight the fire, "Why would they be helping them?"

"I don't think it's the humans helping the goblins," Darragh answered, "I think the goblins were hired." The goblins were

136

hurrying to the far side of the camp to barrels of water and then into the woods.

"Can you tell where they're from?" Ternell interjected.

"From their accents I think they're from the eastern continent; but I'm not sure yet." Darragh became quiet again and watched the clearing tensely, waiting for the right moment.

"Why are they here?" Lorcian broke the silence again.

"I'm not sure. There's no money in burning down a forest."

"But why would they..." Lorcian pressed.

"I don't know yet!" Darragh replied, pulling his eyes from the camp to look at Lorcian, "That's what we're here to find out. That's why you're sneaking into the tent, ok?" Darragh continued to watch Lorcian's face, waiting for an answer to a rhetorical question.

"Ya." Lorcian mumbled.

"If the two of you are done..." Chusa mumbled.

The goblins were on the far side of the camp and the humans had returned to the main tent with the dogs. From where they crouched it was hard to tell, but they could see three humans other than the priest, who they lost track of in the commotion of the fire.

"Lets go," Darragh said in a low tone.

They slipped quickly into the camp at the edge farthest from the flames. They crept along the backs of the simple tents with Darragh in the lead. He raised a hand to stop them and drew a dagger from his boot.

A single goblin came around the side of a tent. Darragh reached for him with a quick grab and pulled him close. He covered the creatures mouth with one hand and, with a jerk of his arm, Darragh buried the dagger into the goblins chest.

They paused to listen and be sure no one heard the struggle, then Darragh yanked the dagger free. He laid the dead goblin between two tents to keep him out of sight and then motioned for the others to follow.

Most of the goblins had gathered on the far side of the camp and were passing water to put out the fire; they didn't see the humans leave. As they approached the larger tents Darragh stopped them and peered around the end of the row. It was clear and he turned to his team:

"Ok, Lorcian, prove you've earned that mouth of yours. We'll head in from here and pull the guards as far as we can. Slip around the back and get rid of the priest."

Lorcian nodded and slipped around a tent and was silently out of sight. Darragh looked to Chusa and Ternell who nodded and fell in behind him.

Well fed guard dogs were tethered at the front of the tent and looked to be better kept than the goblins. They sniffed the air and looked toward Darragh, Chusa, and Ternell, but did not bark.

Darragh unslung a crossbow from his shoulder and loaded a bolt, holding another between his teeth. He peaked around the tent to be sure no one was coming and stepped out for a clear shot.

He leveled the weapon and fired, catching the first dog in the chest; the dog went down quickly and quietly, probably dead by the time Darragh pulled the other bolt from between his teeth. Darragh rapidly loaded the other bolt, aimed and fired. The second dog was caught in the hind leg and let out a long howl of pain while Darragh ducked back behind the tent.

"You missed!" Chusa whispered in astonishment as Darragh reloaded. "You don't miss."

"Who said I wanted to kill it? Now get ready." Darragh had another bolt loaded as the three human guards came from the tent and glanced at the dogs. They immediately looked up, drew their weapons, and began to search; though they didn't search for long.

Darragh stepped out and let a bolt fly that landed in the right shoulder of the first guard, a tall man with dark hair. He let out a yell and looked directly at Darragh. While Darragh loaded another bolt the others took action.

Ternell had drawn a large ax with a curved blade and a picked back. Chusa had curved scimitar whose blade was as long as Ternell ax was tall. Both weapons were well cared for and the edges shined in the flickering light of near by fires.

They ran forward and engaged the other two guards, Ternell charged for the smaller of the two. This slight human had two swords and thin armor, but was stronger than he looked; with a quick side-step he dodged Ternell's first ax swing.

The guard who met Chusa was large, almost matching Chusa in size. His head was shaved and he was covered in tattoos of strange, curved symbols. He heaved a spiked club and moved clumsily under tough hide armor.

Darragh turned his crossbow to the black haired man with the shoulder wound. Cocking the bolt back and readying his shot he was taken off guard by a pair of goblins creeping behind him. The first to reach him pulled the crossbow from his hands, the second landed a punch in his gut. Darragh swung to the side and dodged a second blow while reaching across himself for his sword.

Lorcian heard the noise at the front of the tent and took his cue. He slit the tent at the corner, near to the post to minimize exposure, and slipped inside.

The interior was lit with oil lamps and a large drape hung in the center, creating a back room. Lorcian had admitted himself to the personal quarters of a religious man. Icons he didn't recognize hung above a small alter near the back of the tent.

A hasty table had been made out of crates and a rough hewn board was at the far wall. On it were maps and papers Lorcian glanced at quickly. Crates and tree stumps surrounded the table and a mattress was on the floor in the corner. What interested him most was the chest that was poorly disguised by a sheet at the foot of the mattress.

Lorcian heard someone breathing heavily in the front room.

It was a low, raspy breath and conveniently covered his footsteps. He already had his dagger out and moved stealthily to the opening of the curtain. Using the little finger of his off hand he pulled the drape back and peered into the main room.

The light was lower and an old man was listening to the commotion outside. It was the priest; he stood unusually straight for an older man and from a distance it gave the illusion of youth. Lorcian hadn't expected to be killing a man who could be his grandfather.

Lorcian glided through the drapes and took the room in peripherally. There were work benches against one wall and shelves another. There was some dried food, herbs, scrolls, and vials like the ones they had found in the woods. In baskets on the workbenches were small corks.

Near the work benches stood another alter similar to the personal one, but much larger. The icons were the same and stumps and crates were pushed off to the sides. The priest seemed to serve his flock even in the depth of the woods.

A vial had rolled off a workbench long before Lorcian's arrival and he unintentionally found it with his foot. It crunched beneath the sole of his thin shoe and the priest glanced up, the look of a startled animal registering on his face.

"No!" The priest called in fear and raised his hands to the sky. This was not the typical response Lorcian could count on and he hesitated, unsure what has happening.

"Agni! Do not let my work for you go unrewarded!" He called to the canvas above him; Lorcian braced himself.

The goblins' small daggers could not match Darragh's sword, though they kept him on the ground for a few moments. While pinned down by one goblin the other stabbed him in the arms and torso. Darragh summoned his strength and threw off his assailants. Drawing himself up to one knee he pulled his sword and swung at the first goblin, catching it across the chest. The second stabbed at Darragh, missed, and Darragh impaled it on his sword.

Darragh looked up to see the dark haired guard working his way across the aisle between tents. With the goblin body on the sword and the dagger slits oozing blood, Darragh was weighed down and awkward. The guard was baring down on him, slowed with the effort of raising his sword with his off hand.

With a yell, Darragh heaved the body from his sword and raised it to meet the guard's. They held swords against one another for a few tense moments, staring into each others eyes, measuring their strengths and weaknesses, determining the best way to overcome the other.

They were close enough to smell one another perspire. The dark haired man was a few years older than Darragh, though his skin darker and covered with scars. He was clenching his jaw and barring his teeth, chipped from years of fighting and battled. He mumbled curses in an eastern language Darragh didn't know.

The two men would have been well matched if they'd met without injury. Darragh could see this man was a strong opponent and felt the rush of adrenaline; he growled as he increased the pressure in the hilt of his sword.

The guard tried to match him, but couldn't maintain the angle. Darragh set his feet wide and heaved through his sword. The guard toppled to the ground and Darragh swung his sword up and over his head, bringing it swiftly down. The guard moved to block, but was too slow. Darragh pushed through the feeble attempt at defense and brought the edge of his heavy blade down onto the man's injured shoulder with a 'crack'. His chest gave way and the guard was defeated.

Darragh raised his head with a rush of adrenaline, ready to push on. The second guard was dancing around Ternell and the large man still struggled with Chusa. Darragh could hear more goblins coming from the perimeter of the camp, drawn in by the yells from their human leaders. He positioned himself between his companions and the coming rabbles.

As Darragh faced the goblins, Ternell worked to best the two-sworded guard. Ternell's blows continued to swing wide and his ax blade was dusty from landing in the dirt. The quick-footed guard swept behind Ternell and tried to land quick stabs, but his blows glanced off Ternell's heavy armor.

Nearby, Chusa was locked into combat with the large, brutish human. Both had discarded their weapons, with a preference for hand to hand combat. Their hands were clasped and they squeezed and grunted at one another, testing angles and grips and moving one another back and forth slightly.

They grunted, growled, and flexed in an intricate dance. Chusa enjoyed the challenge for a few moments; it was rare a human could match him and he was pleased to meet this specimen.

While the other two guards were from regions he didn't recognize, this man looked more local. He had sandy colored hair, and when he was ordering the goblins around Chusa heard the familiar accent of Naynor.

"Welcome back to your home country. You much have traveled far for all those tattoos; they're not normal for your people." Chusa taunted him with a grin.

"Shut your mouth, filthy lizard. You don't know anything about my people." The tattooed man spit back, grunting and flexing.

"I know that they wouldn't like what you're doing here."

"Ha!" He scoffed in Chusa's face, "You have no idea what we're doing. We're cleansing this filthy forest and you're just in the way. Agni wont allow it…"

Chusa could hear Ternell grunt in frustration and decided it was time to move on. Chusa gave a toothy grin and chuckled.

"Is that so?" he said, playfully while his opponent gave a questioning glance. "Then I couldn't do this."

Chusa gave a throaty rumble, opened his jaw wide, and broke through the guards hold; reaching his sharp, chipped, dripping teeth toward the guards exposed face. The tattooed guard yelled and pulled his face back and to the side, burying Chusa's exposed teeth into his shoulder. They pierced his leather armor and he howled in pain.

Chusa held the guard in his jaws and the force of the maneuver toppled them both. It successfully broke their hold on one another and, as they parted, blood trickled from between Chusa's teeth and down the guard's chest.

The guard heaved himself up onto his knees, red with furious energy. He surged with anger, grabbed his club, and yelled loudly. To the human the bite was unsporting; though it was a typical attack in drasta fights. Fueled by his hate of the drasta, he threw himself at Chusa. Chusa rolled and dodged the club, tumbling to his feet. He shifted, carefully putting himself between the barbarous guard and Ternell.

The guard smiled broadly.

"My turn to chuckle, filthy dragon." He straightened up and stepped in, his vision sharpened with adrenaline and fury. He raised the club with an awful grin.

"Not so fast." Chusa breathed deeply, roared, and flexed the glands in this throat.

A foul smell permeated the air as Chusa coated the guard in a gooey, acrid liquid. The tattooed guard screamed as the secretion seeped into his fresh wounds and began to eat away his face.

Chusa took no enjoyment in the mans suffering and swept forward, scooped up the club, and finished him with a quick, aggressive swing.

145

He turned to find Ternell dodging the dual swords of the remaining guard, while Darragh worked to pick off stray goblins returning to the tent.

Ternell saw Chusa approaching behind his opponent, and swung wide to the left of the guard. This last guard, thinking he was quick and clever, stepped deftly to his right; unknowingly putting himself between Ternell and Chusa.

Chusa reached forward with is large, claw-like hand and connected with the side of the human's head. The guard struggled to stand for a moment, trying to keep the surroundings in focus. That was enough time for Ternell to swing with his ax and send him sprawling on the ground.

The once-quick guard sensed his own defeat and tried to crawl away. Chusa bared down on him, but he raised one of his swords to keep Chusa at bay. He stood on shaky feet, blinking away the early affects of a fresh concussion.

He turned to run, but after one quick step a crossbow bolt streamed past Chusa's left ear. Chusa jumped at the sound and turned to find Darragh, a pile of dead goblins in front of him, with his crossbow raised toward Chusa.

"I didn't hit you." Darragh said with a shrug. Chusa looked back to the remaining guard to find him stopped and standing, a crossbow bold lodged between his shoulders. The guard fell forward to the ground and lay motionless.

Darragh, Chusa, and Ternell looked from one to the other. Each had a few wounds, though none of them severe. Darragh pulled a salve from a pouch on his waist and quickly smeared it

146

across the slits on his torso and arms. He threw it to Ternell who looked down to find a gash on his arm. Ternell nodded his thanks, dipped in two fingers, and covered the gash.

Darragh started toward the tent flaps and on his way by he ended the whimpering of the wounded dog.

It didn't take long for their eyes to adjust to the new light, though the change in temperature was sudden and obvious. Candles, unlit at the alter, were melting to indistinguishable blobs with the increased heat. Standing before the alter, with his arms and face raised up, was the priest.

His face was red with both effort and warmth, and the heat seemed to channel through him in waves.

"Agni. Greatest of the gods, do not spurn your steady servant. Strike these unworthy nonbelievers."

The temperature in the room was rising quickly and the sides of the tent had begun to brown and curl. Lorcian, standing at the drape opposite the entrance, was making his way though the stumps and crates across the room to the priest.

The priest turned from the alter toward Lorcian and swept his arms above his head. He bent his elbows and swung his arms down and pushed his hands away form his chest. A wave of heat danced from his fingers and the air around him seemed to melt.

It happened so quickly Lorcian didn't have time to react. When the wave of hot air hit him the hair on his face singed and his clothes ignited. It knocked the breath from his chest and for a moment he reacted completely on instinct; dropping to the ground, writhing, and screaming for help.

The others took a step toward Lorcian, but the priest turned to stop them with his hands at the ready.

"You can not defeat the followers of Agni. Aerydae will not be hindered by your simple swords." He raised his arms upward and called loudly, "Agni, grant me your power again!"

The priest swept his arms forward again and a fresh wave slammed Chusa and Darragh. They were further away than Lorcian, and though the force was diminished with distance, they still stumbled. Chusa choked trying to breathe the hot, thin air. He was dizzy and lightheaded, struggling to keep the room in focus and to keep from passing out.

Darragh felt the singe of the hair on his face and hands burning in the heat and he gritted his teeth and squared his feet. Lorcian was calling from across the room for them and they were all determined to save their young friend.

Ternell was surprised to be unaffected. He had braced himself for the impact of the wave and expected to roast in his metal armor; but the impact never came. He could feel the room continue to heat but continued to breath normally, his armor cool against his skin.

The priest turned back to the alter and called to his god.

"AGNI! Reward your loyal servant with the power to finish

them." The priest's face reddened and the temperature rose further. The edges of the drapes and tent walls were scorched, some were igniting, and Ternell's companions continued to struggle. Lorcian had rolled enough to extinguish himself, though was unable to stand.

Ternell did not remember making the decision to attack. His years of training had taught his body to fight as naturally as breathing. He gripped the handle of his ax, raised it, and charged forward. The priest turned and pushed the built up heat of Agni toward Ternell. Both were yelling and under the force of the wave Ternell faltered for a single step.

"De ah hachk!" Ternell yelled in dwarven and heaved the ax above his head. With a wide swing and landed a blow in the priests outstretched left arm, bringing him to his knees.

"Fire god!" He sobbed. "Do not desert me! Fell this unworthy dwarf!"

The priest feebly swung his good right arm toward Ternell and a diminished wave of heat rippled out. Ternell took little notice of the passing attack as he gripped the handle of his ax. In the surge of adrenaline he overcompensated and swept the weapon just above the priest's sagging torso and stumbled as he took off the priest's upturned head. He stood a moment, trying to process what just happened.

The heat immediately dissipated and Ternell shivered with the sudden drop in temperature. Regaining his senses, he ran to Lorcian and checked he was still alive. Not far away Chusa helped Darragh back to his feet.

"Ternell..." Darragh called through dry lips.

"The lad is alive. He's hurt badly, though."

"How did you...?"

"I'm not sure."

Darragh and Chusa joined Ternell at Lorcian's side, and were surprised when Ternell began to chuckle.

"I think the heat may have finally gotten to him." Chusa gruffly whispered to Darragh with a look of concern. Ternell waived them off.

"Remind me to buy a drink for Faye." Ternell reached up his sleeve for the silver chain, "I thought she'd worked some Nixie magic on me to buy it." He dangled the cooling charm toward Darragh, "She told me I would need it, but I thought it was just good to have on tha road..." He shook his head and smiled, "I think we'd be dead now if it weren't for her."

Darragh gave Ternell a nod and a pad on his shoulder, then returned their attention to Lorcian.

"Do you think we can move him?" Chusa asked Darragh.

"I'm not sure – we'd better wait for Jak."

Ternell stayed with Lorcian while Chusa climbed the hill to wait for Jak and Orla. While he was gone, Darragh searched the tent. The alters contained little of value other than the idols to Agni: statues of flaming horses, offerings of silver and berries from the forest, and lamps of perfumed oils. Darragh had no interest in these.

The work benches held another dozen completed lightening vials which he wrapped carefully and slipped in his pack.

In the priest's quarters Darragh found a locked chest, a few bags of coins, and maps of the forest. Under the mattress were letters Darragh scanned, but had little time to examine. He rolled them and slid them into a leather tube to look over later.

Chusa returned with Jak and Orla. He had explained what they missed and Jak breathed with relief to see Darragh safe. After a quick greeting Jak attended to Lorcian.

Jak took the jar of salve from Darragh and pulled small jars of herbs from his pouch. He blended, crushed, and mixed them with the salve and carefully dressed Lorcian's wounds.

"Will he be alright?" Orla had witnessed death before, but it was always the elderly or sick; she'd never seen someone die from a fight. The last few days had been intense; she fought to keep her emotions under control.

"We need to search the camp." Darragh turned from the injured teen to Chusa and Ternell, "The guards had to have something to heal themselves. Search their tents. If you don't find anything, look for the goblin shaman's tent. Bring anything you find to Jak."

Orla looked to Lorcian and Jak and felt helpless; she didn't want to search and Darragh hadn't asked her to. She wandered out the front of the tent and tried not to look at the bodies of the guards, dogs and goblins. Inside was the dead priest and she felt like there was nowhere to go to escape the death and stress.

She looked beyond the tents where Chusa and Ternell searched and saw a small group of trees forming a natural half-circle. It was grassy there and the sun warmed the little patch. Orla was drawn to the spot and knelt there, praying to Danu that Lorcian would survive.

The tents of the guards were stuffy and poorly lit and though Ternell and Chusa took their time, the first tent had a cot and little else. The second had tools for sharpening and maintaining the weapons, a cot, and some traveling supplies. In a small chest among the supplies were two healing potions which Ternell hurried to Jak. Orla saw him heading back and followed, anxious for news of her friend.

In the main tent, Jak eased Lorcian's head back and poured the potions in.

"These are not very strong. If it is safe we should stay here tonight and move him to the Irwu village tomorrow."

"What if the goblins come back?" Orla asked.

"We'll post watches. We can find cots in the other tents and move them here. Ternell and Orla, move the body of the priest outside and then go get the cots. Chusa and I will move the rest of the bodies to the treeline."

Orla didn't want to touch the priest, but didn't want to contradict Darragh either. She did as she was told and readied herself for another hard night.

Chapter Twelve

The night in the goblin camp was long. Orla wasn't able to sleep and stayed up most of the night with whomever was on watch. In the morning they built a stretcher out of tent poles and canvas to carry Lorcian through the woods. He was stable, but recovery would be slow until they were able to reach a magic healer.

Moving through the woods carrying Lorcian was hard and it took over a week to reach Ni'Ca. From there Jak and Ternell brought Lorcian to Naynor where the elven healers could stabilize and mend him. Chusa refused to go, not wanting to deal with the ridicule of the citizens of Naynor, and Orla didn't think she could be much help. Darragh returned to Mithe with them to meet with the city council.

After a few days Darragh found Orla in a freshly tilled field.

The air had turned crisp and cool in the weeks since they left and it would frost soon. She was sitting on a large flat stone and concentrating to mold the dirt with her mind. As Darragh approached she raised a large square of earth, moved it forward and dropped it down to create a short wall. She squinted her eyes and focused on pushing it over, away from herself and back to the hole it came from.

"That could prove useful." Darragh called, not wanting to startle her too badly.

"Ya. But it's not as fun as this one." Orla squinted, raised a few clumps of dirt, and molded them into poorly-made dirt statues of animals. They began to break apart as she spoke. "They won't hold together though."

"Very nice. I have something for you." Darragh produced a purse. Orla peeked inside at a small pile of coins and a few small gems. "Your fee for the Irwu wood; you did an excellent job." Darragh motioned for her to follow and started toward the river. The day was clear and crisp and likely to be the last nice one of fall.

"Thank you. Were you able to find any proof in the camp? Are the drasta cleared?"

"Yes, there was a lot to work with in the main tent. The priest was called Rihall and their were maps of the forest that incriminated them. There were also some of cities on the coast, and a few places on the eastern continents."

"Why was he there?"

"The maps show many places where fires had been set and

there were letters with instructions; and a guide with pages in our language and in goblin on how to make and use the vials to set the fires." They'd reached the water and Darragh stopped and looked into it. "Do you know anything about the god Agni?"

"No. My clan are followers of Danu..." Orla trailed off. Since beginning to attend Eolas she no longer prayed every day, though she couldn't say why. The only time she had prayed was when she thought Lorcian would die. "...I don't know if I am a disciple of hers anymore."

Darragh made a gentle hum and continued to watch the water pass.

"I know few wizards who keep their faith. It's as if being granted the magical gift convinces them it wasn't given to them by a god."

Orla shrugged and stared out as well. She hadn't thought much about why she stopped praying, she only knew that her heart was no longer in it. She changed the subject.

"What was in the letters?"

"Very little of it was personal and mostly from the name he mentioned when cursing us: Aerydae. From her instructions, it seems they were setting fires near thieves' encampments; they just didn't care if the Irwu were nearby. And they had a chest full of money to bribe the goblins with; most of them were for hire and not followers of Agni.

"The letters were signed with a Nixie family seal." He turned and waited for Orla to look up. "I'm sure you realize why this is disturbing."

156

"The Nixies are very powerful..." Orla ventured, "...specifically, they're magically powerful. If they're attacking the other races it would be very bad for everyone."

"Exactly. I've shown the seal to Faye and she verified that it is Nixie. She recognizes the seal, but insists that Agni is not a Nixie god." Darragh turned back to the water. "She's right. It's a human god..." Letting his thoughts drift Darragh continued in a distracted tone.

"Nixies are secretive. Faye isn't going to tell me anything more about this family or their seal... but why would a Nixie be worshiping a human god?"

"Maybe it's a trick." Orla cut in. Darragh looked up from the river skeptically. "Its as likely as anything else. Maybe it's a fake."

"Orla, its not so easy. You will learn to trust that almost any item a Nixie has created will have magic. Even something as simple as the seal on a letter will have magic in it so it can be recognized as legitimate to another Nixie. Faye didn't just confirm for me the family; she confirmed that it was *magically* authentic."

"Oh... Well, maybe the worship is the fake."

Darragh lifted his fingers to the place where his eyebrows had been before the priest burnt them off. "Tell that to the priest."

They walked along the river wanting to chat but having little to say. Ternell had sent word that Lorcian was healing well and would be home soon.

Orla was, of course, worried for her companion, but she

had also worried for Mirna. Orla had volunteered to be the one to tell her what happened, not wanting to take a chance on Darragh's manners when delivering bad news. Lorcian was Mirna's nephew, and when his mother passed away she became responsible. It was hard to see her so upset, pacing with worry; she loved him dearly and if someone else was able to run the inn she would have been on a horse to Naynor as soon as she knew.

Orla had done what she could to comfort her friend. They sat up at night after the last guests went to bed and as Orla recounted the adventure. She spent extra time focusing on Lorcian's discovery of the glass and how it led to them finding the goblin camp, leaving out the details of her visions.

Darragh stopped and Orla returned from her mental wandering.

"There's only one thing to do, though we'll have to wait until after winter."

"What's that?"

"We'll have to find the Nixies; and I want you to join us."

In another week Lorcian and Ternell returned with the last of the large caravans. Ternell refused to let Lorcian ride and insisted they rent a cart. With the caravan came the last of the new goods to be stocked for the winter and the last of the trade, and they were just in time. According to the Almanac the first great storm of the year would come the next day.

Orla hurried out to greet her friends. Lorcian was limping and showing off his new scars with pride and Ternell stood back and laughed. His bragging was interrupted when Mirna came running from the inn. She hugged her nephew and couldn't help to simultaneously praise him for a job well done and scold him for being hurt. Mirna swept him away to a hot meal and a warm bed; Ternell followed, anxious to return to the comfort of his own space.

With her friends gone Orla turned her attention to the merchants. When they were fortunate enough to have a shop dealing their wares the merchants could unload anything the shop was in need of. For goods that were less in demand, or higher value, the travelers would set up their own booths around the market.

Typically, Orla would have avoided these gypsy peddlers. She had little use for fancy jewelry or trendy cloaks. Today was different. Today she had the pouch full of gold that Darragh had given her and knew exactly what she was looking for, if she could find it.

The first four carts yielded nothing. Orla dug through mound after mound of poorly embroidered cloth, jars of dusts and sands for spell work, second hand armor and cheap used books.

The fifth and final cart was more promising. The owner had more discerning taste and carried specialty items. Orla picked through decorated daggers and some small polished pieces of armor before she saw it and her mouth went dry. A polished wooden case, thin and light, with a small silver latch. She peeked inside for confirmation and tried not to be too excited while talking with the merchant. Though Orla was never good at bartering, she managed to get a fair price.

She turned to go, and in her haste walked right into Jayna.

"Hello." He chuckled and grabbed her shoulders to keep her from tripping.

"Hi." She gasped in surprise at their proximity but didn't pull away.

"I've missed you at the enclave and Maeve told me you'd returned."

"Oh... yes. I'm sorry I haven't come to see you yet." Orla's eyes wandered, not wanting to meet his gaze. The truth was she'd been avoiding him on purpose, only visiting the enclave when she knew he was asleep or elsewhere. She was still a married woman and he was very handsome.

"Well, I'm here now." Jayna stepped back and motioned to a low bench in the square. "Come and sit with me. Tell me about your adventure. I've heard from others in the village and what they say can not possibly be true."

Orla squeezed the handle on the case and decided it could wait. She had missed Jayna's company and it was safe to sit with him outside in the square.

Time passed quickly as she told him of traveling on the busy merchant road, the Irwu tribesmen and their round language, the goblins and fire bombs and finding the camp. She blushed through her blunder of setting the woods on fire and missing the signal and teared up describing how she thought Lorcian would die.

Jayna was an excellent audience, gasping at the right times, chuckling when she set the fire, and becoming quiet when she talked about Lorcian's injuries. He even reached out and touched her hand when she was upset.

"Incredible." Jayna let out a sigh as she finished, "And I thought the rumors to be far-fetched. If I didn't know you were honest I'd swear you were exaggerating."

Orla looked at the cobblestones.

"For some parts, I wish I was."

"You should be proud of how far you've come."

Orla blushed. Suddenly the cuffs of her sleeves were very interesting and with this complement she wasn't able to do much more than mumble, "Thank you".

Jayna shivered. The sun was setting and the temperature dropping. "Hmmm," he licked the tip of his finger and lifted it up.

"Should be about right." He stood suddenly.

"Right for what?" Orla watched him stand, walk a few paces, and then return.

"Right for this." He raised his right hand, wiggled his fingers, and his face bloomed into a wide grin as it began to snow. "A present. For your safe return."

Orla gasped and giggled looking up to see the snow forming out of mid air a few feet above them. A ten foot circle of snow was falling just around them.

She stood to meet him and glanced around them.

"You can make snow..." She breathed gently to him.

"Yes. I have something important to tell you." He leaned close to Orla and heat spread all over her as he whispered in her ear, "I'm a wizard." Orla laughed aloud and shoved him away; partially at the joke, partially at her own reaction of him so close.

"Ha! Very funny."

She could have left any time. She could have gone back to her room, but she liked being with him so she stayed a while longer. To keep her distance and distract from her blushing face she stooped and scooped a handful of the wet snow and threw it at him, catching him in the shoulder.

He laughed and played. They threw snow and talked a while longer until after it was dark and a young wizard had come to light the lamps.

 Epilogue

Finally alone, after hours in the cold, Orla warmed the basin of water in her room and lit the fire in her hearth. She plugged the draft in her window with thick a bit of cloth, changed quickly to her night shirt, and climbed into her warm bed with the case in her hand.

She pulled her feet beneath her and set the case on the bed before her. She undid the little silver clasp and opened the lid. Inside the case, lined with black linen, were different minerals and stones; each separated into their own little nook. She moved her hand over the open case and brushed each stone with her fingertips.

The first day after returning to Mithe, Orla had gone to see Maeve at the enclave. She slipped in the doors in the early morning hoping to avoid the other students.

163

Maeve was in her office and anxious to hear about Orla's trip. She described it quickly and paused when she reached the scene in the field. This was why she'd come to see Maeve: the visions she'd had with the crystal vials.

She told Maeve about the visions, about how she'd focused on the vials and could see what had happened with them.

"Why? I understand about the minerals you gave me. Does this mean I can focus it? How does it work?"

Maeve paused to think, wanting to answer each of Orla's questions completely, and Orla watched her working it out in her mind.

"It seems your gift has taken a unique form. I had intended to explore your vision in the spring; though you have done it for us on your own."

Maeve's smile seemed proud and so different from the expression when she and Orla had first met. "I told you before how natural elements can help you focus your power."

"Yes." Orla reached to pull the amethyst from under her shirt.

"Good. I'm glad to see you're wearing it. As you've learned yourself, other minerals can be used to focus on different things. No mineral will show two seers the same thing. If I were to hold a magnetite I would see something different than you would.

"As you've also learned, if a crystal is shaped and used we can focus on what it was for and learn about it. These can also be wiped clean, as I have done with the minerals I gave you, to keep

164

you from seeing how it was used for me."

Orla had stayed with Maeve long into the morning to discuss different uses of this skill and how to focus her energy.

Now she was on her bed and in the case a dozen small stones; some polished and some raw. She wasn't sure where to begin. As she pulled the amethyst above her head she unconsciously held her breath. She set the amethyst down on the top of the case and felt the vision fighting at the back of her mind. Orla let out a hard sigh and reached for the first stone, a light blue topaz with smooth edges.

Her mother! Beautiful and young. So small and graceful. She was smiling and dancing at a festival, clapping and twirling. Orla was seeing into the past. A handsome young man, her father, bowed before her and asked for her hand. They both smiled and swung around.

Orla set down the blue stone and moved to a polished opal, beautiful with iridescent sparkles on its shined surface.

Herself; walking the streets of Mithe. The scene could be any given day. She was well fed and clean and the sun was shining. It was a beautiful day and she seemed happy and strong.

She dropped the opal, anxious to move on. Next was a near iridescent aquamarine.

Jayna. Tall and handsome. Playing by the river and pulling water from it. He turned the water to ice and molded it to a beautiful sculpture in the sun.

Orla felt herself warm to see him playing in the sun and

know that in the vision he could not see her watch him. Maeve had told her that minerals could be used together and she was excited to try it. With a coy smile to herself, she reached down for the opal as well.

They were together: Jayna and Orla standing by the ocean. They were facing one another on a rocky outcropping while the water played below them. She could smell the sea air and feel the wind shifting around her. He reached a hand out and up to meet her face and the other around her waist.

Orla didn't hesitate at all. She slipped her arms around his back and pressed her cheek into his hand. She lifted her face to meet his gaze and moved closer...

Orla dropped the stones and let them fall to the tray below her. *How could I do that Cian?* She took a few breaths to focus herself. *No. I wouldn't! That can't be right. I must be doing it wrong.* She dismissed it completely, refusing to recognize the part of her that wished it was true.

She looked down to the case, anxious to go on but afraid of what else she might see.

She got up from bed to get a glass of water. She paced the room and after a few moments also got a glass of wine from the cabinet. The room was warmed by the fire and between the heat and the wine she was able to push the scene from her mind and return to her bed.

Orla wanted to continue. There was one more person she needed to see.

There were still nine stones left and Orla could feel herself tire with the effort of the visions. She would only have enough energy for a few more. She moved her fingertips from stone to stone waiting to feel strongly toward them. She paused over the clear halite and lifted it. Before she could even close her hand the vision came strongly.

A woman. The woman from her visions only younger. Around her was a beautiful city high in the trees and everything seemed to glow. She was surrounded by noise and excitement, but she was to the side. Alone. Feeling left out. She was so sad in such a beautiful place. She seemed strangely familiar, though not from the other visions. Orla wasn't sure why she recognized her.

Orla set the halite down, unsure what it all meant. She paused a few moments to reflect and then continued. She stopped again over the dark green malachite, the last in the case. She looked down at it and reached for her wine. She swallowed the last few drops and lifted it to her hand.

A tear began to brim as she saw him. *Cian. Soft and gentle. He was in a lantern-lit room and he looked tired. It was stuffy and warm and he was sweating. There were others there with him, though she could only see Cian.*

A woman was crying out and he was comforting her. His face was gentle and he called her sweet and intimate names.

Orla reached forward and moved the case to the floor. She laid down without releasing the malachite or the vision.

"Push. It will be over soon." He said. The woman was in labor. Orla began to cry. *Is that me? Is this what I can't remember?* She

167

could only watch and wait to see. He gave words of encouragement and Orla heard the unseen woman cry with effort.

The others in the room celebrated and the baby cried. **This can't be my baby. My baby died.** The wadima assisting the birth announced it was a boy. Cian smiled broadly and tears began to stream from his eyes and fall from his quivering chin. Someone handed Cian the baby and he looked down into the eyes of his son. Cian smiled down at the baby and then held it close.

Orla wasn't able to hold the vision any longer. She let the malachite drop to the bed next to her, trying to keep the vision of Cain fresh in her mind, and rolled her head into her pillow to cry until she was able to sleep.